King of New York 5

**Lock Down Publications and Ca$h
Presents
KING OF NEW YORK 5
A Novel by _T.J. EDWARDS_**

Lock Down Publications

P.O. Box 944
Stockbridge, Ga 30281

Visit our website @
www.lockdownpublications.com

Copyright by T.J. Edwards
KING OF NEW YORK 5

Lock Down Publications
Like our page on Facebook: Lock Down Publications
@
www.facebook.com/lockdownpublications.ldp
Cover design and layout by: **Dynasty Cover Me**
Book interior design by: **Shawn Walker**
Edited by: **Mia Rucker**

T.J. Edwards

Stay Connected with Us!

Text **LOCKDOWN** to 22828 to stay up-to-date with new releases, sneak peaks, contests and more…

Thank you.

Submission Guideline.

Submit the first three chapters of your completed manuscript to ldpsubmissions@gmail.com, subject line: Your book's title. The manuscript must be in a .doc file and sent as an attachment. Document should be in Times New Roman, double spaced and in size 12 font. Also, provide your synopsis and full contact information. If sending multiple submissions, they must each be in a separate email.

Have a story but no way to send it electronically? You can still submit to LDP/Ca$h Presents. Send in the first three chapters, written or typed, of your completed manuscript to:

LDP: Submissions Dept
P.O. Box 944
Stockbridge, Ga 30281

DO NOT send original manuscript. Must be a duplicate.

Provide your synopsis and a cover letter containing your full contact information.

Thanks for considering LDP and Ca$h Presents.

T.J. Edwards

Prologue
Showbiz

When I stepped into Vorsky's office on Wall Street with Bruno Gomez just a little bit behind me, I couldn't believe my eyes. First of all, the office was very spacious and clean. It had all sorts of paintings by Leonardo Davinci all over the walls. His desk had a pink laptop and a pink box of Kleenex. Vorsky met us at the door with a handshake that was less than firm. He had jet-black, wavy hair, shaved on the sides, and big blue eyes, with makeup on to cover up his blemishes, I guessed. He was sharply dressed in a Burberry business suit with matching loafers.

In his right arm was a little white dog that was the size of a poodle. The dog also had on a Burberry outfit, and its paws were covered with Burberry doggie shoes. I was taken aback because I was expecting some vicious Russian thug with a scowl across his face. Instead, I was met by this cheerful person with very little bass in his voice.

"You must be Juanito Vega?" he asked, shaking my hand. I noticed that his nails were manicured and covered with clear polish.

"The one and only. It's a pleasure to meet you, Vorsky. We have a lot to talk about."

He walked behind his desk and sat his dog in his lap, rubbing its fur. "Not really. Your brother killed my older brother. Somebody needs to pay for that. You need to tell me how you are going to convince me not to have every living Vega massacred." He lowered his eyes and looked over to Bruno. "Oh, where are my manners? It's good to see you, Bruno. You look like you've gained a little weight."

T.J. Edwards

Bruno shrugged his shoulders. "I've been doing a lot of traveling and haven't had a lot of time to hit the gym. Hey, but what are you gonna do, am I right?"

I was sitting there in my chair fuming. I couldn't believe the introduction of this bitch ass Russian. I felt like he'd just threatened my whole bloodline. "Damn, that fucking Tristian." I thought out loud.

"Well, Juanito? I'm waiting?" Vorsky asked, crossing his legs. I sucked my teeth and looked into his eyes. There was mascara around them. "What are you looking for?"

"I find it hard to believe that Bruno hasn't clued you in on my interests." He looked over at Bruno. "I am looking for land. Land is greater than money. You have five hundred acres. I want half or we go to war. Half and the life of your brother."

"You want two hundred and fifty acres of our Vega's land. Are you fucking kidding me?" I asked, feeling my heart pounding in my chest. Looking across at this muthafucka, I couldn't see any threat in him at all. He looked more feminine than masculine. I felt like giving him two to the dome right then and there, but Bruno and I had checked our guns in at the door.

Vorsky smiled and continued to pet his dog. "Well, excuse me, Juanito, but we are in New York. You must always start the bid high. I am open to listening to your counter. Go ahead, darling, wow me." He batted his eyes and smiled brightly.

"Yo, don't be calling me no fucking darling. I got respect for you, Vorsky. Let's keep this shit on a name by name basis, none of that pet shit. Nah mean?"

"Oh, I see that somebody is a little homophobic. Sure, we'll see things your way. Go ahead and present me with your proposal. I'm all ears, Juanito."

8

I was trying to keep calm. I felt like this muthafucka was mocking me or something. And it wasn't that I was homophobic, I just wasn't cool with a man calling me no fucking darling. Shit, I'd never been with a female that called me that, so it was weird. Nevertheless, I wasn't about to have this dude calling me anything but my name. Point blank period.

"I'm not willing to give any of my family's land. But what I can do is give you a life for a life, and twenty five million dollars for the inconvenience. I didn't have shit to do with your brother being killed, but I'm willing to compensate you anyway, just so we can squash this bullshit."

"Unfortunately, you're not offering me anything that I want, other than your brother's life. A piece of your land had to be a part of the equation, or we go to war. It's as simple as that, and please do not let the soft spoken demeanor fool you. If we go to war, you will lose in a bloody fashion, and so will your innocent loved ones. This will be the biggest mistake that the Vegas have ever made. It is in your best interest to play ball with me. This I can assure you of." He smiled and placed a tuft of hair behind his ear.

The last thing I wanted was to go to war with this Russian. Bruno already told me how powerful he really was. I was still in the beginning stages of building up my army of savages. There was no way I was ready to go to war with a billionaire mad man, who probably had something to prove to the rest of the underworld because of what had taken place with his brother.

I had to put my ego to the side and use my brain. And my brain told me that losing some of the land was better than losing it all. There was a season for everything, and this wasn't the time nor the season for me to pick a fight with a nation of real killers.

"Fifty acres of land. You do with it what you please, but your men don't overstep that fiftieth acre of land barrier."

"One hundred acres and you take the life of your brother. I want you personally to bring me his head on a platter and present it before me. There is always room for a little sibling rivalry. Wouldn't you say, Juanito? In exchange for this display, I will not only wipe the slate between you Vegas and us Putins clean, but I will also help you take your family's business global. There's only but so much money in the United States. You have to start to think euros and yens. Pretty soon, the American dollar will be worth the same as a peso. Trump is an idiot."

I exhaled through my nostrils. "Yo, you reaching for a hundred? How about we make it seventy five and I give you ten million."

"I've said what I'll accept. Anything less than this is a loss to me. You can either shake on this deal, or we can make further arrangements."

He picked his dog up and allowed for it to lick his lips. He kissed the dog in the mouth, and I'd had all that I could take. I couldn't believe I was about to be hoed by a person that kissed his dog in the mouth and spoke softer than a woman. I was heated and wanted to kill something.

I extended my hand. "We got a deal, Vorsky. Long as you hold up your end, I'll do the same."

He shook my hand with a limp wrist. "That is very wise of you. I would like your brother executed first thing in the morning. I'd like to have his head on a platter right here on my desk by tomorrow afternoon, around lunch time. Make it happen."

***

I stayed up the whole night with my back against the bathroom door, shooting heroin. I was so fucking mad when I got home, I didn't know what to do. I couldn't go at the Russian directly because he'd have me vanquished. I was sure of that. Tristian was surrounded by old world bodyguards from Havana, so it was going to be a task going at his ass. I had a bunch of things to figure out before the morning, and the only way I knew how to free my mind was by the help of Mrs. Heroin.

So I got fucked up all night until I passed out on the floor of the bathroom with the syringe laying on the floor right next to me. Before my eyes closed, I'd come up with the perfect plan of attack. I would make sure that Tristian's head was placed before Vorsky just as he'd requested. Only then could I move forward with my life and get things on track.

***

"Showbiz. Showbiz. Baby, what the fuck is going on? Are you okay in there?" Kalani screamed, beating on the door. "Showbiz!"

I jerked in my sleep and opened my eyes in a frenzy. My head was pounding worse than ever. I rushed to the toilet and purged my empty guts inside of it, retching like crazy.

"I'm good, baby. I'm just sick." I felt like I was on fire, like I had on three sweaters, even though I was shirtless. Sweat was all over me.

"Baby, I think I fucked up. I need you to come out here or I'm about to lose my mind," Kalani hollered. "Please!"

I flushed the toilet and gargled some Scope, spitting it into the sink and running the water. I washed my face with a towel and opened the door.

Kalani stood on the other side of it with her eyes wide, tears running down her cheeks. She had blood all over her Prada blouse.

"Baby, I got her. I got the lil' bitch. Now I wanna kill her. I need you to stop me from killing her, baby, please." She held a long serrated knife in her left hand. There was blood dripping from the blade.

My inner forearm was itching like crazy. My bones felt like they were cracking, and my head was pounding. I needed a fix. I couldn't fully focus on what she was talking about until I got right. I brushed past her and dropped to my knees, sticking my hand under the hotel mattress in search of my product, and found none. There should have been at least an ounce of Vega heroin there. I was about to flip out.

"Kalani, where is my dope, baby? I'm sick. Where the fuck is my shit?"

"Baby, I got a little girl in the conjoining room. I've already started working on her. I swear I don't want to kill this little girl. You have to stop me." Sweat poured from her face in rivers. Her eyes were glossy. Her hair was all over the place. She was shaking like crazy. I could tell that she was beyond high.

"Kalani, what little girl are you talking about? And where is my shit? It ain't under the bed. I'm sick, baby." My stomach muscles tightened up on me. I hunched over, looking up at her. She ran and opened the door that led to the other room that was connected to ours.

"Brittany. The little girl that got shot the same time your son and Maine did. She took Tristian away from me. It's her fault. I'm gon' finish killing this bitch, bae." She ran into the other room and straddled the little girl with the knife in her hand. From the distance, I could see that Brittany's mouth was duct taped.

12

"Where the fuck is my dope, Kalani?" I felt all under the bed until my fingers came upon the plastic wrapper the dope had been in. I pulled it out and saw there was nothing left inside of the bag other than a few crumbs. I sucked my finger and the saliva on my digits helped the crumbs to stick to my finger. I stuck it up my nose and snorted as hard as I could, searching for some relief from my withdrawals, but receiving none.

"Bitch, you did all my dope. I'm finna kill yo ass," I snapped, struggling to get to my feet. I dry heaved and fell to my knees. I crawled across the floor. My vision was blurry. My hearing distorted. I felt like I needed to shit and throw up at the same time.

"I'm finna kill this lil' bitch, bae. I'm so sorry. It's her fault. It's her fault, daddy," Kalani hollered from the other room.

My phone began to buzz from the dresser top. There was a pounding at the door. I felt like my heart was about to burst. I couldn't breathe. I squeezed my eyelids tight and took a deep breath. I crawled to my phone and read the face. There was a text from Blackie, saying they were ready to handle business, and all of our troops were in place.

Kalani stepped back into the room with blood all over her. It dripped off of the knife. "I'm so sorry, Showbiz. I can't take this shit no more. I can't let you do me like this." She raised the knife over her head and rushed at me with an ear-piercing scream.

***

Tristian

It had been two weeks since I'd sat down and had the meeting with Kosov, and the Russians were still in our land down in Havana. I felt that Kosov was ready to go to war over our land, and so was I. The only problem was that if I had to wage war with the Russians and go at them full force while they were set up in the fields, I ran the risk of damaging a lot of the crops, and therefore not being able to fulfill any orders from the mid-western parts of the United states, and those orders were keeping the Vegas afloat. I had to find a way to get Kosov and his people off of our property without ruining our crops. So, three weeks after I sat down with him out in Los Angeles, he decided to meet me at the W hotel in downtown New York.

When he walked through the door of my penthouse suite and extended his hand, this time I neglected to shake it. Instead, I remained seated while Javier led him to the couch, away from me. I was doped up on twelve Percocets with my heart beating faster than I ever remembered. My face was numb and my throat was completely dry. There were five of the old school guards behind me, with Shapiro sitting to the left of me.

Kosov had a wicked smile on his face. "Mr. Vega, to what do I owe such an honor?"

Two of his big, beefy looking bodyguards stood behind him with their hands in their jackets. Their eyes scanned the room. I could tell they were on edge.

Javier closed the two doors and walked further into the big suite, standing behind me. I mugged Kosov for a long time. I hated the look of his face. I had visions of melting it away with bullet after bullet. I cursed the day my father had gotten involved with such a crook.

The toilet flushed and Showbiz opened the door to the bathroom and walked into the room, drying his hands on a white towel. "Is this that pretty muthafucka, Kosov, that I'm hearing so much about?" He walked over to Kosov with his hand extended.

"The first born." Kosov curled his lip and frowned. "I will not shake your hand. You're nothing to me. Your father didn't have enough regard for you to hand you his seat. The look of your face disgusts me." He waved him away and crossed his legs. He was a cocky muthafucka. I could tell that he felt that the world should be kissing his ass on a daily basis. "Why have you summoned me, Mr. Vega?"

Showbiz plopped down on the couch and clenched his jaw off and on. He bounced one foot on its toes and couldn't stay still. I could tell he was heated at the utter disrespect from Kosov.

"Your people are still on Vega's property. The deal was for me to pay you fifty point five million dollars and our debt would be washed away. I've done my part. Why are you neglecting to send your troops away?"

Kosov sucked his teeth and shook his head. "I've changed my mind. After consulting with the Russian Federation, I decided to completely take over the Vega's fields and make them official Russian turf. In exchange, my Federation will pay you a sum of two hundred million US dollars. After this, you will be ordered to evacuate our land immediately."

"You got to be the dumbest white man in the world. What part of any conversation that we've had thus far has led you to believe that I am interested in selling even a piece of our land?" I moved to the edge of the sofa. My palms began to sweat.

"I no longer care what you want, Mr. Vega. You have no say in this matter. The decision has been made for you. The Federation has already claimed that land for its own. It'd be wise for you to step back and let this happen, or else I can't imagine all of the things that are about to take place against your family." He shrugged. "I prefer murder over giving away two hundred million myself. So, we can play it any way you want." He growled and leaned across the table.

Showbiz upped two .45s that were already cocked, put both of them to Kosov's forehead and stood up. "You see, I ain't like my muthafucking brother. I don't scare so easily. You sitting here talking all of this tough shit about what you and your people gon' do to me and mine. How about I just leave yo' fucking brains on the table right here and right now, white boy?" He pressed both barrels harder into him.

"Mr. Vega, tell your brother to stand down. This will only make matters worse. I am Kosov Putin. Nobody does this kind of shit to me," he snapped, hollering through his clenched teeth.

The bodyguards behind Kosov had their guns aimed at Showbiz. My troops had their weapons aimed at his. Javier upped a .9 millimeter off of his waist and aimed it at Kosov. I remained seated.

"Fuck you, Kosov. I ain't telling him shit. Let's see yo' tough ass get out of this one." I sat back on the sofa and smiled.

"Get yo' punk ass on the phone and tell them Russians to get off of our land, or I'm putting two in your head, and we'll take it from there," Showbiz hissed.

Kosov looked up at him and lowered his eyes. "You think if you kill me that you're in the clear? Huh? Is that what you think? Well, let me tell you something, that land is as good as gone already. You're fighting for a lost cause. Once the Russian Federation wants something, they take it. Look at what they've done to your White House. The Vegas aren't as important or as powerful as the Presidency of the United States. You want me to call and tell them to retreat? Well, I'll tell you to kiss my Kremlin ass. You filthy ni—"

Boom. Boom. Showbiz's gun jumped in his hand and sent two bullets into Kosov's forehead. "Bitch ass cracker."

Kosov flew backward and wound up bloodied against the leather sofa with his eyes wide open. Half of his face had been removed.

Javier shot from a silenced .9 millimeter. His bullets connected with Kosov's guards' heads. They jerked on their feet before falling to the ground. "Are you crazy, Juanito?" He put his pistol back on to his hip and stepped into Showbiz's face.

"What the fuck are you talking about, Javier?" Showbiz asked, mugging him.

"You've just waged the worst kind of wars. The Vega's didn't need this kind of drama. This one act may have not only cost us our land, but it may be the end of the Vegas as we know it. Fuck!" He looked over to Kosov's bleeding body.

Showbiz stepped away from him and looked down at Kosov. "That white muthafucka wasn't about to give us our fields back. You heard him. He tried to treat us like a bunch of bitches. I ain't with that shit. I sent his punk ass on his way, and I'ma do it to every last one of them Russian bitches if I have to. Shit ain't sweet. So fuck what you talking about."

"That's it. I've had enough of your mouth, Juanito." He grabbed Showbiz by his shirt and punched him in the mouth, knocking him over the table. Showbiz's head hit the side of the couch. Javier jumped over it and pulled him up, punching him again in the nose. He made his head slam into the floor before he pulled out his .9 and pressed it to Showbiz's cheek, cocking the hammer. "Say your prayers, Juanito. It's time that we're rid of this plague that is you." He placed his finger around the trigger ready to buss.

Showbiz blinked repeatedly, all dizzy like. He looked into Javier's face and squinted. Blood ran from the back of his head and pooled on the carpet. "Kill me, bitch. If you don't kill me, I'ma kill you," he promised through gasps.

Javier held him down. "That's it." He bit his bottom lip.

Boom. Javier's head jerked forward before he fell off of Showbiz with his brains oozing out of his skull. Showbiz wobbled to his feet and looked down on him, staggering from one foot onto the next. I stood over Javier with a smoking gun. I felt sick to my stomach and wished I'd never had to kill my uncle, but I had no other choice. He had been seconds away from killing my brother. Even though there was bad blood between me and Showbiz, I refused to allow anybody else to take his life. I felt that when it came down to it, I would be the one that sent him to the Reaper. I wasn't letting nobody steal that privilege away from me, not even Javier.

Showbiz raised his foot and stomped Javier in the face, repeatedly.

* * *

Shapiro arranged for the entire crime scene to be cleaned up and the bodies disposed of. About four hours later, I watched Javier's body being tossed piece by piece into the Hudson, just as Miguel's body had been.

Showbiz placed his hand on my shoulder and shook his head as we watched from the limo. "Yo, kid, I know you feeling some type of way about wasting that old nigga, but had you not, he would have killed me, son. I love you for this. Word is bond, I ain't ever gon' forget that."

I waited until my crew loaded into their trucks before signaling to the limo driver for him to pull off. "You know what, Showbiz? I don't know what the killing of Kosov is going to bring unto our family. Whatever it is, I'm ready to die fighting it because I am a Vega until my last breath. Now, when it comes to Javier, I'm sick over that kill, Dunn. That was Pops' brother. He was a good man. You shouldn't have provoked him the way that you did. But it is what it is, though. We gotta move on and figure this shit out before we become victims of the underworld."

Showbiz turned up his bottle of Hennessy, drinking half of the bottle. He stopped and wiped his mouth. "I love you, kid. I know you don't think I do, but I'm letting you know now that I love you as much as my cold heart will allow. I didn't give a fuck about that old geezer. I didn't give a fuck about that Russian, and had you not taken care of Miguel, I was gon' slump that nigga, too. My heart is black. I'm fucked up in the head. All I care about is being king of this family. I'm willing to do whatever it takes. I'm willing to kill anybody that I have to in order to obtain my birth right. That shit eats at me every single day." He turned the bottle back up and swallowed it in big gulps.

I watched him closely. He looked like he'd lost another five pounds. He was still muscular, but there was definitely something off about him. I couldn't quite put my finger on it. "You know what, Showbiz? Maybe I ain't the man for this throne. Maybe it is supposed to be rightfully yours. I mean, I ain't seeing what you're seeing. All I'm seeing is a bunch of problems that can't be handled without falling deeper and deeper into the abyss. I want more than this, kid. I always have."

Showbiz nodded. "Then give it to me, nigga. If you saying you don't want to be king of our family any longer, then denounce your throne and hand it over to me. I'll show you how to reign supreme as a true Vega, against all odds. That's my word." He sniffed and pulled on his nose. "I'ma need access to everything you got right now, though. The factories, the fields, and all the money. I'm hip to the off-shore accounts, too. I'll let you keep a nice amount, but for the most part, I'ma need 'em all. It'll be my right to have as king of the Vegas."

I nodded. "Give me a few days to think about it, and I'll let you know what's good."

He smiled. "Nigga, take a month. It ain't no rush. I gotta be out of town for a minute anyway. I got some important people to meet up with. Them Russians ain't the only heavy hitters in the foreign world. In order to destroy an enemy, the Vegas must align ourselves with the enemies of our enemy. You feel me?" He took another swallow from his bottle.

I didn't give him a response to that. But that night I stayed up into the wee hours of the morning tooting pills one after the next. I couldn't believe I had killed my own uncle. A man that had stood behind me one hundred percent. I shed tears as I rocked back and forth in the den of my mansion, with Biggie rapping in the background. Life was starting to get the better of me. It was to the point where I began to question the purpose of the Vega's throne. To sit upon the throne meant that I would never be able to be happy because there would always be somebody or some family gunning for me and my family. It would never end, and I was already tired of it.

***

A week later, Showbiz appeared at the front door of my mansion with red eyes and a bottle of Hennessy in his hand. "I fucked up again, Tristian." He took a swallow from the bottle and belched real loudly.

I grabbed him by the shoulder, looking behind me to make sure that neither Brittany nor Perjah were anywhere within earshot of our conversation. "What the fuck are you talking about, Showbiz?" I looked him up and down. He smelled of alcohol and must. His long hair that was usually kept nice and neat was unkempt and all over the place. His breath smelled funny as well.

He shook his head. "Yo, I understand why I'm so fucked up now, kid. It's my son. I ain't ever been able to grieve over him, and I had to do what I had to, Tristian. You gotta understand where I'm coming from." He tilted the bottle and started to take a series of gulps from it. "I ain't mean to do what I did. Not to her, but I had to. It's the only way I'm gon' be able to grieve, kid." He scratched the inside of his forearm and I could see the needle marks.

"What the fuck are you talking about? You did what to who?"

Perjah came down the stairs in some tight pink boy shorts with the matching pink wife beater. When she saw that I had company she made her way back up the stairs. She stopped at the top, covering her crotch area and her breasts. "Baby, when you have a second can you come up here so I can speak to you?"

I nodded and waved her off. "Yeah, bae, in a minute. Let me see what's the matter with my brother."

"Okay, daddy, but please, whenever you get the chance. It's important." She disappeared down the hallway.

Showbiz rubber necked, looking up the stairs. I thought he was trying to see my baby's ass and that pissed me off. He grabbed me by the shirt and balled the material into his fist. "I fucked up, Tristian. You gotta forgive me. But if Maine ain't no more, then she shouldn't be either. My son was my everything. I had to avenge him. You gotta see where I'm coming from." He pushed me back and opened the door to my mansion. He stopped and looked me over before stepping out into the daylight.

I squinted, not understanding what he was talking about. I jogged to the door as he drunkenly got into the driver's side of his Wraith. "Showbiz, who the fuck are you talking about?"

He pulled his leg into the car and slammed the door. He started the engine and revved it by stepping on the gas. Then I saw the window roll down. "Tristian, don't hold this shit against me, boss. Remember, I'm your blood. That's thicker than water." He peeled out of the driveway with the bottle of Hennessy turned up. I watched smoke waft from his tires as he sped away.

I stood there in the hallway scratching my head. "What the fuck is he talking about?" I asked out loud before shaking my head. "That nigga gotta be bugging right now. Word up." I closed the door and made my way upstairs.

Perjah was sitting on the edge of our bed, rocking back and forth with a .45 in her hand. "Is he gone, baby? Did you tell him to leave our home?" she asked with wide eyes.

I frowned and closed the door behind me. I knelt in front of her and took her manicured hands into mine, kissing the backs of them. "Baby, yes, he's gone. You're safe now. Do you hear me?" I sat beside her and pulled her into my embrace.

"He's the devil, Tristian. Every time I see your brother I feel like I'm in hell. He's evil. I've been having a lot of bad dreams about him." She blinked tears. "He's going to hurt one of us, baby. I can feel it."

I frowned and held her tighter. "I'd never let nobody hurt you or Brittany. I already told you that. Speaking of which, where is my daughter now?" I asked, looking around as if she was in the room.

"She spent a night with her grandparents. She'll be there until Sunday afternoon. Don't you remember me telling you that?"

I shook my head. I couldn't for the life of me remember us having any conversation about Brittany going anywhere. I shrugged and kissed her on the cheek. I could feel her body shaking. "I don't remember you telling me that, but if you're saying that you did then I won't put it past my selective hearing. But I want to talk to her to make sure she's good."

She nodded and stood up. "Let me go and get her grandfather's new number off of the counter. I just wrote it down last night and forgot to add it to my phone. I'll be right back." She stood up, placed the gun on the bed, shivered, and walked out of the room.

My phone began to vibrate on the dresser. I grabbed it and put it to my ear after answering it. "What's good, Shapiro?"

"Boss, have you heard from anybody back in Havana lately?"

"What? N'all. Not since a few days ago, why?"

"Tristian, the Vega's mansion was under heavy fire the last I checked. The fields have been set ablaze. I haven't been able to confirm who the attackers are, but I have reason to believe that it is the Russians. I need to meet with you as soon as possible. There is only one move we can make to squash the beef with Kosov's people. But I won't say it over the phone. I'll be there in an hour. I'm on the jet."

My head was spinning so fast. "Alright, Shapiro, keep me in tune, man. I'll keep trying to get a hold of some family from down there." I hung up with him and called my mother. The phone rang and rang, but there was no answer. I sent her a text, telling her to get back to me as soon as possible. I spent the next few minutes calling and texting as many of my family members in Havana that I knew. I was unable to receive a response from any of them. I felt like throwing up. The world was spinning so fast.

Perjah walked into the room with her hand over her mouth. She shook her head. "Tristian, not my baby, again. Not my baby, again, Tristian. Please God, not my baby, again." She fell to her knees and dropped the phone. She was carrying, screaming into her hands.

I rushed to her side on the floor. "Perjah, what are you talking about? Where is Brittany? What's the matter with you?"

I removed her hands from her face. Before she could open her mouth to say anything, there were tires screeching to a stop in front of the mansion. I heard multiple doors opening and the sounds of boots on the gravel before the shooting started. *Boom-boom-boom! Boom-boom-boom! Boom-boom-boom!* Our attackers began to chop at the mansion.

Perjah covered her ears and screamed at the top of her lungs as the windows to the mansion shattered. Bullets chopped into the walls repeatedly. The old school Cubans ran toward the front of the mansion with Choppers in their hands before they began to shoot back at the enemy. The walls were being picked apart. Smoke clouds of drywall puffed into the sky as more and more bullets flew in our direction.

I laid on top of Perjah, shielding her from the storm. I had to protect her with everything that I was. I vowed to never let her reach harm.

She screamed in my ear, shaking uncontrollably. "My baby, Tristian. He killed my baby." Her eyes rolled into the back of her head before she fainted.

Chapter 1
Showbiz

"Showbiz. Showbiz. Daddy, wake up. Why are you sleeping so hard?" Kalani nudged me enough to cause me to buck my eyes wide open. Before I could make a move, she slipped on top of me, and straddled my body. Her brown eyes peered into my own. She had a broad smile on her face.

My head was killing me. I squinted my eyes. She'd pulled back the electric blinds, causing the sun to shine directly into the room and it was fuckin' me up. "Yo, get ya ass up and close them blinds, shorty. My head pounding like a mafucka."

"Dad-dee, guess what day it is?" She leaned further into my face and kissed the tip of my nose.

"Yo, on my mother, if you don't get yo' ass up and close them mafuckin' blinds, we about to have a serious problem. Do what the fuck I say," I yelled.

Kalani hopped off of me and grabbed the remote control off of the dresser. She hit the button and the blinds began to slowly adjust until the room went dark. The Aquarium along the back wall illuminated the room with its blue light. Two baby sharks swam inside of it. She stood at the foot of the bed with her hands on her hips and popped back on her legs. "Daddy, don't tell me that you forgot already."

I sat up and grabbed the platter of Vega heroin off of the night stand. It was already separated into eight thin lines. I took two the hard way, one up each nostril, and set the platter back down. "Yo, you know I got a million things I am doing. What the fuck am I supposed to have remembered now?" I wiped my nose and drank from the warm bottle of Moët. It tasted horrible.

Kalani poked out her bottom lip. She stomped her foot, and slowly made her way back to the bed. "Daddy, are you playin' wit' me right now? Do you really not know what today is?" She stood before me dressed in a short white t-shirt that stopped just above her thighs. She flashed her bald pussy lips every time she moved in the slightest. Over the last twelve months she'd gotten thicker. The weight looked good on her.

"Kalani, you already know we ain't finna do this. I ain't about to play these games with you. Tell me what it is and we'll go from there." I slid my hand under the pillow.

She stomped her foot again. "That's fucked up. I remember everything that you tell me to remember, but you act like it's so hard for you to remember when my fuckin' birthday comes around. It's only once a freaking year. Damn, Showbiz." She sat on the edge of the bed and crossed her arms.

I pulled the box from Tiffany and Co. from under the pillow and tossed it at her back. "You gotta start giving me more credit than that. Remember, you're my mafuckin' baby girl. Bitch, I made you."

Kalani turned around and stood up. She mugged me, and then picked up the box. Her eyes lit up. "Dang, you always playing wit' people. I knew you couldn't forget my birthday. I'm dat bitch, fuck Lizzo." She opened the box and took out the three carat, princess cut, pink diamond ring that had cost me fifty thousand. She held it up in the air, and then closer to her eye. "Aw hell nall, nigga. This doesn't look like it ran you nothing more than sixty. I appreciate it and all of that, but you ain't finna sell me short, I'm ya mafuckin' jewel. Where is the rest of my birthday gift at?" She replaced the ring and closed the box loudly.

I stood up with my piece hard as hell, and stretched. "First you finna get on my ass because you thought I forgot your birthday, now you getting on me because fifty gees for a present ain't enough. What the fuck you want from me, Kalani?"

"Nigga, fifty thousand ain't nothin' when you seeing millions. I've been beside you every step of the way, even when you were down and disgusted, strung out and shooting that shit up your arm. Now that you're making major moves and slowly taking over New York, I want my rightful due. You already fucked up my birthday morning by waking up and cursing me out." She tossed the ring box at me. "What else did you get for me?"

I mugged her and stepped into her makeup-less face. Even without it, Kalani was gorgeous. "Who the fuck you think you talking to, huh? You think cause I've been letting you sleep in this mafuckin' bed beside me that it gives you the lead way to be acting all stuck up and cocky?"

"You muthafuckin' right it does. Now what's good?" She closed the distance between us and bumped her chest into mine.

I laughed and pushed her ass on the bed. She tried to bounce back up with a serious mug on her face, but I was on top of her. I yanked her shirt upward and around her stomach. Then stuck my hand between her thighs. My fingers played over her thick sex lips.

"Get off of me, Showbiz. I hate you right now. You're so fuckin' selfish. Get off of me," she screamed, kicking her legs wildly and beating at my chest.

I held her down with my weight, and found her opening. Two fingers slipped past her folds and sunk deep into her warm center. Before she could get used to the intrusion, I was running them in and out at full speed, causing her juices to flow out of her.

Kalani tried to clamp her thighs together. "Stop it. Stop, Showbiz. Get the fuck off of me. I ain't feeling you right now."

I got between her thighs and positioned myself perfectly, lined my dick up, and slid into her with one stroke. Her nails dug into my back. "Bitch, I own you. I fuck you when I want to. I don't give a fuck who birthday it is." I bucked forward hard.

"Unnnnnh! I hate you. Get off of me, please." She beat at my back with her little fists.

I slammed forward and pulled back. Her sex lips sucked at me. I plunged harder, and then I was fucking her li'l angry ass like a savage, digging deep while I sucked and licked all over her neck. Her earlobe wound up in my mouth, before my tongue dipped inside of her canal.

"Unh. Get off me, daddy. Unh. Unh. Unh. Fuck. Shit, daddy." Her thighs opened wide. She laid back with her mouth open. I licked all around her lips, and wound up sucking on her bottom lip. "Daddy, please." Her eyes rolled to the back of her head.

I watched my dick go in and out of her bald pussy. Because she was light skinned, her golden lips were turning a dark brown due to my pounding. Whenever I pulled back too far, her inner pink flashed, and then her back would arch. "You my mafuckin' baby girl. Daddy wanna hit this pussy, daddy gon' fuck this pussy. You hear me?"

She shivered and screamed. She slapped my face, sat up, and bit me on the chest. "I hate you, daddy. I hate you." She shuddered and fell back on the bed, shaking like crazy. Her tongue traced her lips again while my dick plunged into her faster and faster. She screamed, closed her eyelids tight, sat up, and then threw herself backward, cumming hard. I could feel the jets of her pussy shooting at me. I was seconds away from cumming myself. "No." She pushed me as hard as she could, and slid from under me. She jumped up and ran off of the bed.

I tackled her to the floor. She landed on her stomach. I pushed her right knee to her chest, and slid back inside of her. I grabbed her hip and fucked her as hard as I could. Our skins slapped together loudly. Her nail dug into the carpet and scratched at it. "This my pussy. Mine, bitch. You belong to me. Tell me you know. Tell me," I growled. I opened her thighs and dropped into her middle, over and over, sinking deeply.

"Daddy. Daddy. Awwww. Fuck. Daddd-eee. I know. I know. Fuck, I know," she grimaced.

I pulled her up to her knees and got to fucking her from the back while I smacked that fat ass. Every time my hand crashed into the flesh, it jiggled. Kalani was strapped. "Daddy, finna cum. He finna cum, like momma. Slam this mafucka back. Give it to me."

Kalani laid her face on the carpet and slammed her ass back on my dick at full speed, over and over. Her tongue traced her lips, and then she was sucking on her bottom one. "Awwww daddddyyyy!" She came again at the same time that I was cumming. We collapsed to the floor, I fell on top of her back, pumping and nutting deep inside of her, shaking and biting on the back of her neck. She moaned loudly, twitching, and working her inner pussy muscles, milking me.

***

"Oh my God. Oh my God. Oh my God. Daddy, you didn't," Kalani screamed, running out of the mansion with bare feet. She nearly broke her neck crashing into the 2021 pink and black Bentley truck that was sitting on the matching rims, with the Fendi leather interior. Her name was stitched into the headrests, and the license plates read: Spoiled. She threw open the driver's door and climbed inside, flashing me and two of my security guards, obviously not giving it a second thought because she was so consumed by her birthday gift.

"You remembered. You remembered, daddy. I told you I wanted one of these trucks a year ago. How did you remember?" She started the truck, and stepped on the gas. It roared with a low hum.

I walked further into the sunlight with my Gucci robe tied around me, my flip flops were Fendi. I was naked underneath And the crisp spring air made me feel good. "Yo, I had to wait until they started making these mafuckas. I wasn't about to get you no old shit. These mafuckas ain't even supposed to come out until the end of the year. I promised the insider that sold me this that I wouldn't allow for the tires to hit the pavement until at least August. You think I'ma be able to keep that promise?"

She glared at me. "Hell nall, it's yo baby girl birthday. I'm finna get fresh and we gon' break this pretty bitch in tonight. Aw, daddy, you got me so happy." She jumped out of the truck and looked it over. The white bow that was wrapped around it glistened in the sunlight. She did a full revolution before she walked into my arms. "I love you so much, daddy. I swear I do."

I laughed. "Yo, when I was all up in that ass a li'l while ago, you was sayin' you hate a nigga. Now you love me. You are as bipolar as me." I hugged her to my frame.

She held me for a moment and then looked up to me. "Showbiz, I'm fa real, I love you, and for my birthday, I wanna hear you say it back."

I slipped from her arms, and adjusted my robe. I had to squint because it was so bright out. "Don't fuck up ya day, shorty. You already know how the god feel about that love shit. It ain't in me. Now I'm rocking with you the long way, and that's all that matters. You my mafuckin' baby, fuck love."

She frowned. "Fuck that." She poked me in the chest with her index finger. "Nigga, you gon' love me. I ride beside yo ass day in and day out with my life on the line. I'm loyal. I do shit to you that I never thought I would do to any man, and I accept shit from you that I would never accept from anybody else. You gon' love me. Now say it."

I clenched my jaw, and leaned further into her face. "Once again, fuck love. You my li'l bitch, and I'm fuckin' wit you the long way. You riding a Bentley truck and you got a few hundred thousand in your bank account from fuckin' wit the king. Bitch, you are a Vega Blood. That's love. As far as that other shit go, fuck that, and fuck you of you keep fishing for it. I would rather kill you in cold blood than to say that weak ass shit. Fuck love." I grabbed her by her throat. "Do you hear me?"

Her eyes got bucked. She slapped my hand away and rubbed her neck. "Yeah, I hear you. I hear your crazy ass loud and clear." She pushed me out of her face and rolled her eyes. She stepped back in front of her Bentley truck and smiled. "Yo, which one of those hoes in New York riding cleaner than the Queen of the Vegas? None, that's who." She hopped back in her truck and closed the door, turning her music all the way up so that it vibrated the ground.

While I was on my way back inside, Blackie came rolling down the long driveway in his black Cadillac Escalade. He pulled up in front of me and jumped out. "Say, kid, we got a major problem. We need to talk like asap." Blackie was my number one hitta. He was like the top general of my Vega Blood army. All war strategies and plans of attacks were run by him before I moved forward.

"Say less. You wanna roll around and get an understanding, or you wanna come inside and kick back?" I asked, taking another step toward the entrance to my mansion.

"Yo, we should roll so I can show you what the fuck I'm talkin' about. But just to give you a preview, it looks like the Vegas are about to have some serious problems out in New York when it comes to our money and narcotic flow." He shook his head.

"Oh really? Why the fuck for?" I turned to face him fully, stepping down toward him.

"You ever heard of the Coke Kings, a deadly crew of savages ran by some nigga out of Harlem named Kammron?"

"Kammron? What about Kammron?" Kammron was an old rival and enemy from Harlem. He was a street nigga and jack boy the last time I'd checked. We'd fought numerous times in school, and he had a better record. I'd never liked him or his right hand man, Bonkers.

"Yo, kid done came back to Harlem with that clout. He shutting down our traps, and trunking niggas. He got the whole borough rallying behind him. He on some next level shit. Son wanna meet with you man to man to get an understanding about the borough. He said if not, then it's going to be an all-out war. What's good?"

I was so heated that I was shaking like a mafucka. The last time I'd heard anything about Kammron or Bonkers, they were barely making ends meet. How the fuck could Harlem be behind them when I was bred in that mafucka, and it was because of me that most of the dope boys were eating? "Say, Blackie, set that shit up. Tell that mafucka we gon' meet like bosses at the Waldorf Astoria, downtown."

"Got you, boss, I'm on that right away. Oh, and I hear Tristian fuckin' wit a trapping crew out of Brooklyn now. I don't know what's good wit them niggas or how much noise they making. Do you want me to find out?"

Tristian wasn't a threat to me. Ever since I'd had Shapiro confirm that neither I nor Kalani had been the one to kill Brittany, he'd kept his distance and I'd kept mine. He called himself dead set on rebuilding the Vegas. In my opinion, the Vegas as we knew them were crushed. The only surviving members of our family were forced to run under me and my crew of money hungry savages.

"Man, fuck Tristian. He ain't a threat. Set this meeting up with Kammron. I need to see what's good. We'll deal with all of that small shit at a later date. Word up." I pulled my robe tighter around me and disappeared into the mansion with my mind racing faster than a whip in NASCAR.

T.J. Edwards

Chapter 2

It was four hours later when Kammron and five of his Coke Kings from the set strolled through the penthouse doors of the Waldorf Astoria. Kammron was a caramel skinned nigga with deep waves and a slim but muscular frame. He stood at about six feet even, and had almond shaped eyes. He always looked as if he were up to something slick. I never liked the nigga, and I knew that I never would.

He stepped into the main portion of the penthouse and stopped. He was dressed in a white and black quarter length Chinchilla with the matching Gucci fur hat, over the same colored Gucci fit, and wheat colored Burberry boots. All of the strings were undone. His neck had so much jewelry on it that it almost looked comical. He had a green blunt in his hand and a bottle of Ace of Spades.

He eyed me. "Well if it ain't that silky nigga, Showbiz. You done finally moved up in the world. It's fucked up that we got our big bags at the same time though, ain't it?" He laughed.

I sucked my teeth and stepped into his face. "Fuck you talking bout? Nigga, you work for Jimmy the Capo. Yo' bag could never be as big as mine. Fuck you thought this was?"

Kammron snickered. "You're so out of the loop that you twisted." He pulled off of his blunt. "Last time I saw Jimmy, that fuck nigga was being cut into a thousand pieces by his own blood. Bitch nigga fish food now. I'm the muthafuckin' boss. This is Harlem." When he said that, his crew pulled their red bandanas over their faces and stood behind him.

That shit ain't pump no fear in my heart. I stepped closer to him until our noses were touching. "Check this out, Blood, ain't no room in Harlem for you Coke King niggas. That mafucka already belong to my Vega Blood niggas. We feeding the slums. We rocking that bitch. Bottom line is, I got plans for my borough. So step."

Kammron broke up laughing. He held his stomach. "You hear this old nigga? Goofy talkin' bout step." He looked back at his crew. Then back to me. "Listen, slime, I was born and bred in Harlem, right on a hundred fortieth and Lennox. Nigga, my mama gave birth to me right there in the fuckin' building. You, on the other hand, yo mixed ass was born in Havana, Cuba. By the time you made it to the borough, I already had my first piece of pussy, sold my first bag, and kilt my first nigga." He frowned his face. "I bleed Uptown, boy. I am Black Heaven. North New York beat in my heart and ain't no islander gon' take shit from the god. I'm willing to die for my borough. So what is you saying?" He took a step back and opened his arms. "I came here to tell you to move around. If not, we about to go to the mattresses."

"The mattresses, fuck you talkin' bout?" I was ready to crack this pussy nigga right in the mouth.

He snickered. "You a goofy. The mattresses mean that my niggas about to mount up and be prepared to get no sleep until we done murked every Vega Blood nigga in existence. After we slay you weak ass niggas, then we gon' rep our land. One way or the other, Harlem belongs to the set. This Coke Kings right here, bitch." He gripped his Ferragamo belt buckle, cocky and arrogant like.

My troops closed in behind me. Blackie made eye contact with me but I could tell he was nervous. I didn't give a fuck. I upped my .45 and placed it to Kammron's forehead. "Bitch nigga, do you know who you talkin' to?" All around the room guns were cocked loudly. Our troops closed in closer to us.

Kammron placed the blunt to his lips, and pulled off of it. "First time a nigga put a gun to my head, I was six years old. Then again at nine, then ten, and again at twelve." He laughed.

"All of them bitch niggas is dead now. We squeeze triggers where I'm from."

"Oh yeah, Fleet?"

He glared at me. "Just like yo time is running short to pull yo pussies out of my borough, time for this meeting is running likewise." He opened his chinchilla and showed me that it was laced with explosives. There was a clock detonator. It was previously set for five minutes and ticking backward. There were three minutes left on the timer. "Yo, like I said, I'm ready to die for this shit. Are you?"

I slowly backed up with my gun aimed at him. "Nigga, you nuts. Fuck is wrong with this nigga?" I looked around the room. Everybody backed away from him with the exception of his crew. They closed in around him. Me and mine headed toward the exit.

"I'm letting you know right now, Showbiz, that it's about to be a war if you don't move around. All yo traps, all of yo workers, them bitches either gon' fall under the Coke Kings, or they gon' cease to exist. We bout that murder shit. Fuck wit it," Kammron hollered. Then he started cursing like he was losing his mind.

All I knew was that the bomb inside of his fur was down to forty five seconds. Me and my Vega niggas broke up out of the hotel, expecting for it to blow up.

***

That night I called a meeting with my top hitmen and sat at the head of the table while ideas were bounced all around the room. Blackie spoke up first.

"Say, kid, that nigga, Kammron, only acting like that because he and them Coke Kings niggas just linked up with some cutthroat Shooters out of Chicago that call themselves the Born Heartless Mafia. Kid 'nem roll state to state on that bodying shit, and Kammron got them on the payroll. Second to that, his potnas over there on Lennox just got a few crates of Dracos and FHN assault rifles. They ready for war. Kammron snatched all of Jimmy's old hittas, and all of his connects. Son money is flowing and he ready to take over some shit."

"Damn, nigga, it sound like you jocking this nigga more than coming up with a solution. The reason I called this meeting is because I need to know how we should go about getting at these Coke King mafuckas. Y'all in the field right now. The god been traveling, getting our overseas shit in order. Any suggestions?" I looked around the table. Nobody was making eye contact with me. They were all looking off, or avoiding my stares altogether.

I grew irate. I stood up. "Yo, so this what it is? You niggas fear this take over a somethin'? Y'all hearts pumping that Kool-Aid shit?" I stopped and looked around, still nobody was looking directly at me. "Aiight, we finna do this shit another way then. Y'all already know I ain't wit' no pussies working under me." I turned to Blackie, "Say, kid, gimme that Glock from yo belt."

"What?" He asked, looking up at me for the first time. Now all eyes were on him.

"You heard what the fuck I said. Gimme that burner, nigga." I stepped around to his side of the table.

He took the gun off of his waist and handed it up to me. "Here you go, kid." He sat back down.

I cocked that bitch. "Awright, niggas and bitches, this is how this is finna go. You mafuckas about to help me come up with a solution or I'm about to get to whacking niggas one by one. That goes to you hoes in the room, too, word up. Now, my first question is, how do we go about knocking off these Coke Kings? Anybody?"

Now the room was looking nervous. One of the sistahs spoke up. "Yo, kid, they getting deeper and deeper every time we turn around, and they strapped. They got better guns than us, better whips, and making more money. That's the reason everybody switching sides, or picking Kammron's side to begin with. I think the only way we can go at these niggas is if we step up our arsenal and the pay you giving us to create a loyal bunch of killas. And then we gotta get on some no mercy, no fear type shit. If we don't, we are about to get wiped out by Killa and his crew, facts."

I stepped in front of the redbone, and looked down on her. She had a chubby face with light brown eyes. Her black hoodie was pulled half way over her head. "Yo, you feeling like you ain't eating enough in my crew or something? Fuck you bring up the pay for?"

She lowered her head. "Look, Showbiz, I ain't taking no shots at you, but you're the only person here that's living in a mansion. The rest of us are living in the projects, or we ain't even got a spot to lay our heads. Kammron getting his soldiers right. He copping them duplexes and condos, paying their rents and shit, and even flipping the River houses getting them up to par. Kid going hard."

"Yeah, and you feel like I ain't, huh?" I squatted down and tilted her chin so she could look into my eyes.

"Nah, son, you do the bare minimum. We ain't eating in this bitch. You getting fat while we starve, word up. All of us repping a Vega bloodline that we ain't got no parts of. Even yo' brother, Tristian, out in Brooklyn feeding his troops better than you feeding us, and he just getting started."

I found myself getting heated. Not only didn't I like the way that this bitch was insinuating that I was handling my people rough, but I couldn't believe that she had enough heart to admit how she was feeling. "Yo, so why are you here, shorty? Why you ain't switch sides like everybody else who graves I'ma be digging soon?"

"Because I'm a loyal bitch, that's why. That pancake shit ain't in me, son. But you were real foul compared to how the other heads treated their peoples. Yo, we wanna ride foreign whips and ball out, too. Mostly everybody in the crew rocking fake ice, except you and Blackie. That shit technical foul."

"Shorty, what's your name?" I asked, standing over her.

"Mecca, and I'm from a hundred and thirty fifth and St. Nick. Harlem to the death of me, word up." She mugged me.

"So what do you propose I do?" I asked, pushing her hood from her face. There was a long scar down the side of it.

"Yo, you gotta feed the killas before they get plotting on eating you. The only thing that sets a successful boss aside from one that is crushed is loyal killas beside and around him. Right now, that nigga, Kammron, feeding his animals bloody steaks, and we getting road kill. Feed the killas nigga, or wind up on the menu. Word to Harlem." She curled her upper lip with her chest heaving up and down.

"Yo, is that how you really feel?" I tightened my hand on the handle of the gun.

"Hell yeah, my family starving like addicts on skid row. We ain't got shit to eat right now. You ain't hitting the workers until Friday, and the way shit going, my money will never make it until then. This pandemic shit is only making things worse. Now we aren't only starving, but we are worried about getting sick. We ain't got no health care. That nigga, Kammron, footing the bill for all of that shit, yo. His outfit prospering because he's investing into his army. That's the way you do shit."

I nodded. "The whole room feels like this?"

Slowly but surely heads began to nod. Mecca stood up. "Yo, let him know what the deal is. How the fuck a boss gon' level up if we don't say shit, word up?" All around the room the troops began to speak their minds, saying the same things that she had been brave enough to say on her own. I took heed. I grew angrier and angrier, but I took heed.

"Yo, check this out, on my word and the borough, I'm finna get all you niggas right. I been bogus and me focused, I'm finna change all of that. Gimme two weeks to get shit in order. Meeting dismissed." They began to get up and disburse. "Yo, Mecca, stay back and let me rap wit' you, goddess."

"No can do, Showbiz. I gotta get back to the projects. My mother gotta be at work in fifteen minutes. I got five siblings to watch." She picked up her book bag and threw it over her shoulder.

"Yo, fuck that. I'ma roll you there. We need to talk bidness. Cool?"

She paused for a second. "That's good, as long as you can have me there before she leaves, it's Gucci."

"I got you. Let's roll."

T.J. Edwards

Chapter 3

When I got into Mecca's project building, the first thing I noticed was the stench of piss, shit, and crack cocaine smoke. All three scents were so strong that I was forced to pinch my nose. Mecca seemed unaffected by it. She pulled her hood tauter over her head and climbed the steps two at time. There was all kinds of litter and rodents in the stairwell. The walls had all sorts of graffiti and insects all over them. There were so many empty forty ounce bottles of liquor that it made it hard to find your proper footing on the steps while going up a few flights. We passed dope addicts, shooting up heroin, and crack addicts with their backs against the wall blowing thick clouds of smoke from their pipes. When we finally made it to her flight, I was shocked that she was so desensitized to everything around us.

She walked to the middle of the hallway and stopped in front of a red door. She looked both ways before taking her key and sliding it into the lock. She paused. "Yo, my moms be illing sometimes, so don't pay her no mind. Ever since my pops left us to fend for ourselves when I was three, my mother just been all over the place. So be smooth." She turned the key and pushed the door in.

We stepped inside. An older woman with a thick afro that was matted to one side, with dark skin, and a slim frame stood up from the lone couch that was in the room. She walked over to Mecca and stepped into her face. She wore a light blue nurse's uniform. "You almost made me late, li'l girl."

"Yeah, but I didn't. You should get there in plenty enough time." Mecca rolled her eyes and walked around the woman.

The apartment was without furniture, with the exception of the couch. There were two pallets on the floor, made by blankets, and four children sleeping on them. The kitchen

43

looked dirty, and everywhere I looked I was able to spot a roach, or a rat, running along the wall, which I found odd because they had a cat walking lazily through the house.

The woman rushed to get into Mecca's face. "Don't bring yo ass in here with no attitude. and if you gon' bring a nigga over here to be fuckin' in my house, you better make sure that he hit me off first." She nudged her to the side and stepped over to me. "Boy, you look every bit of thirty. You can give me fifty dollars to fuck my baby, or you can give me five dimes of that boy. Which is it gon' be?"

"Mama, what are you doing?" Mecca lowered her head and covered it with her hand.

"I pulled out a bankroll, all hundreds. Huh, shorty. This is a buck. Even though I ain't got no intentions on fuckin' kid, this should get you up out of our mix."

She snatched the money and tucked it into her bra. "Un huh. I have seen yo' type a million times. I know my baby built. That's 'cuz she got those southern roots. Louisiana, that all come from my side of the family. Look." She turned around and proved that she'd handed down her backside to Mecca. I couldn't do nothin' but laugh. "Yeah, the proof is in the pudding, ain't it?"

"Mama, you about to be late." Mecca walked over to the door and opened it for her.

Her mother held out her hand. "My name is Medina. If my daughter kinda boring in that bed in the back room, make sure you stick around for me. I know what I'm doing. This Baton Rouge right here." She winked her eye before leaving out of the door. Mecca closed it behind her.

I stepped over to Mecca. "Yo, it's good, shorty. Don't feel no type of way. We can't pick our parents."

She shrugged her shoulders. "It is what it is. Why did you insist on following me back here?" She locked the door and

44

walked into the kitchen and began to clean it up. She didn't even bother stepping on the many roaches that were all over the floor.

I came into the kitchen a few feet behind her. "I liked how you spoke up at the meeting today. A hunnit niggas in the room, and you had mo balls than all of they ass put together. That's rare."

She took a bar of soap and got a towel nice and soapy with it before she proceeded to wash the dishes. "Yeah, well I ain't got nothing to lose. You see how I'm living, kid. I have been fucked up ever since I was five years old. What you see now has been the norm for me. I wish things were different, but they ain't, and it is what it is." Roaches crawled along the dish wringer. There were a bunch of dead ones under it.

"Say Mecca, what is your goal out here in these streets?"

She kept washing one plate after the next. After rinsing them, she placed them in the dish wringer and grabbed another one. There appeared to be an endless supply at the bottom of the soapy water. "I just wanna have my own. I'm tired of coming home and having to deal with this. Ain't nan one of those kids in that other room related to me. My mother gets a check for all of them, and it seems like I'm the one that's raising them. It gets old." She sighed.

"So you saying you're just trying to get money?"

"By any means. Yo, I'm willing to do whatever it takes, too, as long as I ain't gotta sell my soul." She finished washing the dishes and picked up a broom. Now the roaches were crawling all over the floor crazily. She swept the majority of them into a pile, along with the trash, and dumped them into the overflowing garbage that was already crawling with roaches. There were two big rats along the side of it, sniffing and eating trash in their little paws.

"You know what, because of how you handled yourself today, I think I wanna give you a slot close beside me. I need a mafucka that's gon' keep shit gangsta with me at all times, somebody that's not gon' be afraid to tell me when shit looks real fucked up, and what they think I should do about it. Have you ever bussed a gun before?"

She nodded. "I'm from Harlem, kid. You already know, that's a given."

I stepped further into the kitchen. "What about on that murder shit. You got a few under your belt yet?"

She gave me a side eye. "That's confidential, Dunn. I would never ask you some shit like that."

"I can dig that." I looked around the apartment, and shook my head. The cat took off behind a big rat, while another rat took off behind him. They wound up in the back of the apartment out of sight. The cat screamed. There was loud hissing from the rats, and then the cat began to whimper loudly. "Yo, what if I said I wanna move you up out this bitch tonight, would you be wit' it?"

She stopped mid mopping, and looked up at me. "Take me where? To that fancy ass mansion you got over there in the Hamptons?"

"Nall, shorty, just a hotel for tonight. But tomorrow, we can work on getting you yo' own shit. I got a few connects that fuck wit that real estate real tough. I'm sure we can find you something."

She looked past me. "But what about them?" She motioned with her head toward the four kids that were lying on the floor.

"I thought you said they wasn't no kin to you."

"Sometimes I refer to them as my brothers and sisters, but in actuality, they ain't. But I still can't leave them here overnight. What if somethin' happen to them?"

46

I shrugged my shoulders. "Fuck em. All I care about right now is getting you right. You're a Vega Blood."

She looked into my eyes. "What about the rest of the crew? What, you think I'm the only one that's living in fucked up conditions like this? You wanna take pity on me? Huh? Is that it?" She stepped into my face.

I took a step back. "Nah, shorty, I don't do that pity shit. Coming from where I'm from, that pity shit a get you kilt quick."

"Then why are you here trying to remove me from my situation when there are so many other members in our crew starving to make ends meet?" She waved me to get out of her way so she could mop the floor. I stepped back. She took the sink sprayer and sprayed the floor. Then she proceeded to mop it.

"That's why I need to put you in the best position under the Vega Bloods. A position where you'll be able to see that the distribution of funds are used appropriately throughout our mob. I'ma put everybody in place to get some major money. And when it comes down, you gon' make sure that it is evenly distributed amongst the killas of the crew. How does that sound to you?"

"First off, why me? and secondly, how the fuck any of us is about to make some money when you got Kammron slowly taking over Harlem and putting his Coke Kings in place all over the borough? Yo, we lost four of our men yesterday to Kammron's gunners. Happened right over on Seventh Ave, around the corner from One Forty Fifth. I'm surprised none of the fellas ain't have enough decency to tell you that. And I wanted to, but also didn't wanna sound like a big mouth know it all either."

"Yo, it's like I said, you got more balls than most of the niggas in our crew. Do you want this position or not?"

She finished mopping and wrung the head out in the sink. Muddy water came out of it, along with roach particles. "Yo, that's a lot of responsibility. But if you think I can handle it, then hell yeah, Dunn, sign me up. What about Kammron, though?"

"Don't worry about that nigga, for now. I'ma figure that situation out real soon."

***

Kalani was waiting up for me when I got back to the mansion. She had two open duffel bags of money, and was placing it, stack by stack, into a money counter. She wore a short Victoria Secrets nightgown. "Bout time yo ass got back home. That nigga, Tristian, been hitting up my phone all day, trying to get a hold of you. Finally, I told him that if he ain't got your direct contact, it must mean that you ain't fuckin' wit him. Then I hung up on his ass."

"Fuck that nigga. We ain't got shit to talk about anyway. What's good wit' you? Why you seem like you have an attitude and shit?"

She shrugged her shoulders. "Probably because it's my birthday and we ain't do shit for it. I mean, I got a bunch of gifts, but I would've loved it if you would have taken this day to cater to me. I don't ask for much." She counted another bundle while the machine whirred loudly.

I slid beside her. "Yo, bidness been calling a nigga all day. That's my bad that this day crept away before I could even get a hold on it." I picked up a ten thousand dollar bundle of hundreds and handed it to her. "Huh, li'l baby. Happy birthday."

She glared at me. "You think it's all about the money and materialistic shit for me, don't you, Showbiz?"

"Ain't it for everybody?" I wrapped my arm around her neck. "Huh."

She knocked the money out of my hand, and stood up. "I don't give a fuck about this money, Showbiz. I care about you. I like when you hold me. I like when you cater to me, and baby me. That's all I wanted for my birthday, damn. Was that too much to ask?"

There were hundred dollar bills all over my lap, the floor, and the couch. I mugged her crazy ass for a long time. "Bitch, pick my mafuckin' money up or I'm finna choke yo ass out. Pick it up."

"Fuck you. This is my day. You pick it up." She crossed her arms in front of her.

I stood up. "Bitch, I'm not playin' wit' you. If you don't pick up my shit, I'm finna put yo' ass down."

"Fuck you. You heard what I said."

With blazing speed, my hand shot forward and grabbed her throat. I picked her ass up into the air and held her there while her pretty toes beat against my chest. I squeezed and put her against the wall. "I blew more than a hundred thousand dollars on you for your birthday, and you still ain't satisfied. How the fuck you think we supposed to keep making money if my business don't trump this emotional shit? Huh? Huh, bitch? Answer me." I squeezed harder and looked into her eyes until she closed them. She beat at my hand, and then all of a sudden, her body went limp. Her knees buckled. I released her and she fell to the ground. I took a step back to look her over. She was unmoving.

I kicked the bottom of her foot with my own. "Get yo ass up and pick up my money."

She remained still.

"Kalani, get up." I kicked her foot. "Kalani, get up before I smoke yo ass."

Still no movement.

I began to panic. "Aw shit." I knelt down beside her. "Kalani, wake up, baby. Wake yo ass up. Come on, man." I pushed on her chest, and shook her. I leaned down and placed my ear to her lips. I couldn't hear anything. Now I was really freaking out. I began to pump on her chest, administering CPR to the best of my ability.

"Fuck, bitch, wake up. I love yo stupid ass. You hear me, I love you. Don't go. Wake up, shorty." More chest compressions. She didn't move. I stood up and looked down on her. "Fuck, I done kilt my li'l baby." I watched her for a long time until I began to have to fight off those emotional feelings. Then I got ready to leave the room so I could think clearly. I had to get rid of her body. I was a foot into the hallway when I heard laughing. I stopped mid stride and turned around, optimistic.

Kalani sat back on her elbows laughing. "Nigga, I told you that all I wanted for my birthday was to hear you say you loved me, mission accomplished." She climbed to her feet. "I love you, too, daddy. That's all you need to know."

I was so relieved that I had not killed her that all I could do was wave her ass off and bounce from the room, before I choked her out again.

"Long as I know you love me, Showbiz, I can endure anything that's thrown my way," she yelled. "You ain't never gotta say that shit again. Once was enough for me."

Chapter 4

As promised, I went into overdrive to make sure that my loyal Hittas out of Harlem had everything that they needed to be able to stand up against the rival drug crews that fell under Kammron. A week after I'd been over to Mecca's projects, I linked up with Blackie's uncle, Chad, out of D.C. He was an Eighth Ward nigga over that way, and he had ties that reached all the way back to Silk Perry, and Alpo. Blackie spoke highly of him, and out of all of the mafuckas that were looking to distance themselves from the Vegas because of the heat our last name brought forth due to the squashed war with the Russians, Chad was looking to do business.

It was a hot and humid Friday night when me, Blackie, and Mecca rolled into D.C. Blackie trailed behind my two thousand and twenty Benz truck, while Mecca sat in the passenger's seat with a F&N on her lap. Her bandanna was all black, and pulled up to cover half of her face. I was rocking all black Gucci, black jeans, the black hoodie, the black Retro number three Gucci Jordans, and even my frames were Gucci. There was a .40 Glock sitting on my lap, and I had two of my loyal killas from Harlem sitting in the back seat of the truck on high alert.

I had never been to Washington D.C. before for business, and from what I was told by a lot of the real live head bussa from my borough, they were making it seem like the Eighth Ward was where them grimy, cold blood, noodle knockers derived from, and that we had to be on point. I didn't give no fuck about that because I was a cold blooded noodle knocker, and I made sure that my niggas was on that bloody shit before we even left New York, including Mecca.

The goal was four crates of M5's with the invisible beam that only the shooter was able to see. Blackie assured me that

T.J. Edwards

his cousin was one hunnit, and if it turned out to be anything less than that, not only would his cousin and his entire family be crushed, but he would be, as well. When it came to the game, you had to be careful who you vouched for because your word could easily turn into a death sentence.

Chad and three of his homies were standing in the middle of the parking lot when we pulled into their complex, twenty minutes after we rolled into D.C. All of them had ski masks on their faces, and I could tell vests, as well. "Yo, you see how puffy these niggas chests are, shorty?"

Mecca nodded. "Yeah, I see that shit."

"That means if shit goes south, you aim at their mutha-fuckin' head or face. Fuck that body. Understood?" I looked over at her.

"I wasn't aiming for no body anyway, Dunn. This the game of survival. I'm trying to kill a nigga ass dead and keep it moving. We are a long way from home." She slammed the fifty round clip into her gun and cocked it.

I turned to the back seat. "Say, Blood, kid nem rocking vests. So blow their heads off if shit starts looking funny. This is Harlem, word up." They both nodded. I opened the door and stepped out of the truck. So did Mecca, and Blackie.

Chad was a short heavy set nigga with long gray dreads hanging from his ski mask. He extended his hand to Blackie first, and shook it. They wound up giving each other a half hug. Then he walked to the side of Blackie and extended his hand to me. "And you must be, Showbiz Vega? Yo, the world has been raving about you Vega boys. It's good to meet you in the flesh."

I shook his hand. "Why the fuck all yo niggas wearing ski masks? Who they hiding from?"

He laughed. "We ain't got no state system like you boys do back in New York. A mafucka catch a case out here, and

52

it's straight to the feds. All of my niggas done been in that bitch two or three times already. We ain't trying to go back. No flex."

I adjusted my .40 Glock and pat his chest. "And these vests. Fuck you got them on for?"

He looked off. I followed his gaze and saw a few shooters adjust themselves in a tree that was overlooking the parking lot. "We been warring wit them North Philly niggas. Mafuckas think Meek just do that rap shit, but that nigga really cause chaos in these streets. He put two birds on my head and I got three on his. It's a long story that doesn't concern New York."

"Fuck New York, this is Harlem. Let's not get shit twisted. They could blow New York off of the map. As long as Harlem is still standing, I wouldn't miss the city one bit. But that's neither here nor there. Where are we taking care of this bidness at?" I looked around. There were niggas walking up and down the street with their fingers stuffing ear pieces in their ears. Occasionally, they would look over at us, and then act as if they weren't paying attention at all. I found that real peculiar. "Yo, what the deal wit son nem?"

Chad peeped. "They're on the payroll, and we're handling this bidness upstairs over in that row house right there." He pointed before walking off with me beside him. My troops followed on high alert, and so did his. "Yo, I have heard a lot of shit about you, Showbiz, and ain't none of it good."

"I don't give a fuck what you heard. That ain't got shit to do with what we finna do tonight. Shid, I done heard a lot about you D.C. niggas when y'all go to the joint, too." I snickered.

"Touché." He kept walking. "So tell me somethin', god, what's going on in Harlem that you niggas about to need two crates of assault rifles?"

I looked at this li'l chubby nigga from the corners of my eye. "Why you asking so many questions, Dunn? All you need to know is that I'm here. I got yo blue faces, and that's all that matters. Ain't nothin' else important."

"Yeah, I guess you got a point." The parking lot was full of ski masked hittas. Some of them walked feminine like, while the other ones you could tell were men.

The row house looked run down from the outside. And by the looks of the regular people that I had seen so far, I could tell that we were most definitely in a rough area. But once again, I didn't give a fuck. I was ready to do this deal and get back to the greatest city on earth.

Chad led us into the back door of the row house and waited until all of my troops, along with his cousin, were inside. Once we stepped inside, we were led through a narrow hallway, where there were killas on each side of us, as if they were in army formation. All of them had on ski masks, and they held assault rifles in their hands. I was starting to think that shit was becoming overly one sided. If them niggas wanted to annihilate us, and take the money off of our bodies, I don't think we could have done much damage.

"Yo, where the fuck we going, B? You got us all kinds of out of bounds," I asked, not feeling as secure as I had when I first pulled up. I was the head, and the first priority for me as the head was to make sure that my troops were always in a position to win. I didn't feel like we were in that position at this juncture.

Instead of Chad answering my question, he stopped in front of an open door, and looked over at me. "Here we go right here. After you."

I looked him up and down, and then looked back at Mecca, and then Blackie. They eyed me for support. I nodded and stepped inside of the small apartment with them alongside me.

Inside, the room was empty, with the exception of two gray crates in the middle of the floor and two masked gunmen standing behind each one. They held M5s in their hands with silencers on the end of them.

Chad came into the apartment and knelt in front of the crate. "They're all right here, Showbiz. One hunnit percent military issued M5s."

I stepped in front of him. "Fuck you waiting on? Open one of them bitches?"

He laughed and pulled a screwdriver out of his belt. He pried it into the side of the crate and popped the lid. It came open and before me was a box full of M5s. I didn't wait for him to give me the go ahead. I snatched one out and looked it over. I took the clip out and slammed it back in, then cocked it, disbelieving that it was loaded. It felt heavy in my hands. I aimed at the wall slightly tapping the trigger so that the beam appeared. "Hell yeah, this what I'm talking about." I nodded at Mecca.

She took the duffel bag with five hundred thousand dollars and tossed it to me. I held it out to Chad. "Here you go, homie."

He took the bag, and looked inside of it. He smiled. "Looks like our business is done here. It was cool fuckin' wit you, Showbiz. I can tell that you a good nigga, regardless to what New York saying about you and your Vega bloodline." He snickered and walked toward the front door.

I stood there for a minute while my men rushed to pick up the crates. They opened the second one to make sure that it was full of rifles. Upon confirming that it was, they closed it back and carried the crates into the hallway, leaving me and Mecca inside with Chad. "Yo, what you just say about my people, kid?"

Chad stopped and turned around. "I ain't say shit, but why you making it seem like if I did that you are in any position to do somethin' about it?"

I walked up to him with the M5 at my side. "Yo, I don't give a fuck what's good with you, Dunn. Keep my bloodline out of yo' mouth. I am a muthafuckin' Vega, and you don't know what I've been through, me nor my people."

"I don't give a fuck either, nigga. This the Eighth Ward, not Harlem, or Cuba. Ain't that where you really from? Either way, you are a long way from home, son. Mind your manners and roll up outta the projects with your merch. Shit starting to get on my nerves."

Blackie came into the room. "Yo, chill, niggas. Fuck y'all on right now?"

Mecca stepped in front of him. "Yo, when bosses talkin', shut yo mouth. Showbiz got this."

Blackie mugged her. "What?"

"You heard her." I mugged Chad. "Harlem wherever I am, Dunn. I bleed Uptown, and that Vega name rings bells all throughout the world."

"Not in D.C. Fuck Harlem, and fuck the Vegas. Get yo pretty ass outta my building before I drop you like a cigarette butt. Right the fuck now."

Now I was in his face. "Yeah, nigga?"

His four troops closed in behind him. He reached on his waist and got ready to pull out his pistol. It was like everything happened in slow motion. Mecca reached under her shirt and pulled out her F&N. She placed it to the side of Chad's head and pulled the trigger. His brains slammed into my shoulder, bloody meat splashed all across my face before he fell to the ground with his eyes wide open.

Then she turned her gun to Blackie and popped him three times in the face while he stared in disbelief. He twisted and fell on his side, twitching like crazy. Chad's guards were slow to act, but I wasn't. I knelt down and got to finger fuckin' that M5 like new pussy.

Boom. Boom. Boom. Boom.

One by one, his men fell all over each other with big holes inside of them. My Harlem shooters had the crates open, grabbing rifles out of them and taking part in airing out the hallway. I could hear men screaming like bitches in horror movies as they went through wetting shit. I stepped on Blackie's face and kept making my way down the hall. "Let's go, Mecca."

"I'm coming." She bussed her gun all the way until we were out and standing in the parking lot, with the money bag on her shoulder.

The parking lot area was deserted, to my surprise. That caught me off guard because I was ready to splash some shit. My killas rushed the crates to our van and threw them inside of it. Mecca jumped in the passenger's seat of my truck with the bag of money and blood all over her mask. Her chest was heaving up and down like crazy.

"Yo, kid, let's get the fuck back to Harlem. I hate leaving my borough. Word up."

I turned the key and mugged her, while peeling out. "Damn, bitch, why the fuck you kill Blackie?"

"That nigga put us in harm's way. If it came down to some shooting shit, he was gon' choose his blood over us, so I wasted his ass. Stop dwelling, it's all a part of the game. I'm keeping half of this money." She put her seat belt across her chest as I stormed down the street at ninety miles an hour.

"No, you ain't, all that shit yours. You earned it. Blood in, shorty."

"And Blood out." She turned up the music and laid back nodding her head with a slight smile across her face. As premature as it was, I felt a way about her. Mecca was definitely that deal.

Chapter 5

Seeing as we were now strapped and ready for war, I didn't waste no time hitting up Harlem with a vengeance. The first week after we tore off the weapons from D.C., I gave the order for my troops to kick shit off in a bloody way. The command was simple. *Jump in twenty whips and roll around Harlem, looking for anybody that resembled a Coke King. When you spot them, your job is to blow their head off, and move on to the next target.*

It was time that the Vega Bloods took control of Harlem, and that was that. I didn't fuck wit Kammron, and I wasn't about to let that nigga be king of my borough when I was the one that was really ready to die for this shit.

My soldiers followed my commands to a tee. In three weeks' time, the Vega's were responsible for thirty three murders, and only two of them were innocent bystanders. The war was on. In an effort to clap back before his legacy was ruined, Kammron sent his troops at ours with all kinds of fully automatics. And before I knew it, I found myself dead smack in the middle of the bloodiest summer on record for Harlem. Nobody was safe, women were getting smoked just as much as the men were.

The Vega Bloods lost three women at one time one Sunday afternoon when they were coming out of Church. Kammron's killas pulled up, and jumped out of their car. They ran up on three of our women, while they were holding their little children, and blew them down with no mercy, then had the nerve to throw a red bandana over each of their faces before they rolled off into the sun set.

To counter that, I sent Mecca and two of our female shooters into a daycare where I knew that four of Kammron's Coke Queens worked. Mecca didn't say a word. She simply walked into the daycare, and up to the staff that were sitting at the front of the room having lunch, and got to spraying. She bucked her gun until it was empty, and left the daycare with children screaming and blood all over the walls and floors.

Kammron waited until six of our dope boys got to getting hot and heavy playing a full court game of basketball before he allowed two twelve year old females to stand up from the bleachers with assault rifles in their hands. They had been sitting there the whole time, but because they were so little, and looked so innocent, they went unnoticed. They rushed the courts shooting the guns, killing all ten men, only six of them belonged to me. Before the little girls could make it out of the park, they were gunned down, as well, by another crew that sold dope in the area with my temporary permission.

To counter that, two of Kammron's barber shops were gunned down. Four people lost their lives. All four of them were his men. I considered that a mission accomplished. More and more revenge killing took place over the next few months until two little boys that belonged to a Harlem pastor were killed. That's when the community started to cry out and call for a cease fire.

It was at this same time that Tristian showed up at my doorstep with four of his hittas from Brooklyn. When I opened the door, I had a mug on my face. I was already irritated because Kalani was getting on my damn nerves.

"Say, Showbiz, I need to talk bidness, and I won't take no for an answer." He stepped into the doorway, which would've made it hard for me to close the door in his face.

"What I tell you about showing up on my doorstep unannounced and without permission?"

"Well seeing as you refuse to answer my calls, texts, or when I hit you up on social media, this is what I have to do."

He stepped into the mansion, and two of my armed body-guards blocked his path. He looked over to me.

"What is this pertaining to?" I asked dryly. I didn't feel like putting up with this bitch ass nigga. I didn't give a fuck that he was my brother.

"Money and the Coke Kings. I know you been warring with that fool, Kammron, real tough, and I just might know how you can knock his ass off, and take over Harlem. Second to that, I got some information in regards to some major money, and new ventures that you may wanna jump off into with me. I'm talking about millions."

"Yeah, li'l homie, no cap?"

"No cap, all we gotta do is sit down so you can hear me out."

I looked over his shoulder at his crew. "I don't give a fuck what we finna talk about, yo henchmen gotta stay outside. You understand that?"

He frowned. "Nigga, just like you don't go nowhere without your hittas, I don't either. What's all this shit about anyway? You already know how us Vegas get down."

"I don't care about none of that, my mansion, my rules. Kick those Air Max off and follow me." I walked off toward my den. I looked over my shoulder one time to see what he was doing.

He cursed under his breath and began to take his shoes off. I could hear his chains clanking into each other. When his shoes were officially kicked off, he was searched, and then pushed toward me. I snickered and kept it moving. I still couldn't believe that my father had given this nigga the throne over me.

***

After popping bottles of Moët, and passing a jar of Percocets back and forth, I sipped from my Lean and nodded my head in a "what up" fashion to him. "What's good?"

"Awright, let me start from scratch. I been fuckin' around in Brooklyn real tough, Red Hook, Flatbush, Marcy, the whole nine. And ever since I been there, the natives have been showing me mad love, and opening up the borough for me. Money been good, the loyalty to this point has been one hunnit, there has only been one problem."

"And what's that?" I asked, disinterested.

"Bonkers."

"Bonkers? Who the fuck is that?"

"You gotta remember blood. Bonkers was Kammron's right hand man, even when we were back in high school. Them niggas used to steal cars and jack mafuckas together, until Bonkers got hit up, and wound up in a coma."

"And, why are you telling me this? I don't care about kid being in a coma. I barely remember the nigga."

Tristian sipped from his Lean and closed his eyes. I could tell that he was fucked up. "Let me finish. You see, while Bonkers was in a coma, Kammron, was fuckin' his wife-to-be and taking over his drug clientele. He burned the nigga's bitch's salons to the ground and had a baby by her. All of this shit Bonkers don't even know about."

"And, that sounds like some personal shit that they gotta deal with amongst themselves. Why are you telling me this?" I was super annoyed already, and ready to smash Kalani ever since the Percs started to kick in. I got to thinking about how it was going to feel to be fuckin' her li'l thick ass from the back, and I was ready for Tristian to get up out of my mansion.

"Yo, the reason I'm telling you this is because that nigga, Bonkers, is slowly becoming a major dope boy and gunner out there in Brooklyn. His brother, Jimmy, had a whole bunch of

Jamaican mafuckas that rolled behind him before he got killed. Before he died, he gave the order that if anything ever happened to him, everybody was supposed to fall under Bonkers. And while everybody didn't take heed, there were a bunch of killas that did. When you mix those Jamaicans with the soldiers from Harlem that followed him here to Brooklyn, and the savages that's already there, that means that Bonkers has a young army of lunatics."

"Nigga, I do, too. So what's your point?" I grabbed my bottle of Patron off of the table and sipped from it.

"I get that, but if we can find a way to let Bonkers in on this information. He gon' flip. Son gon' lose his marbles, and then he gon' go at Kammron super hard. If he does that it's gon' be easy for the both of us to do what we gotta do."

"The both of us, what are you talking about?" That Patron mixed with those Percocets hit me quick. My eyes lowered, I could feel my body becoming slow and numb. I loved the feeling.

"Yo, since you're doing yo thing over there in Harlem, I have decided that I wanna lock Brooklyn up. The only mafucka that's really gon' give me a problem is Bonkers. There has always been bad blood between us and Jimmy because you and that nigga stayed getting in to it. Y'all made me and Bonkers box on numerous occasions, and that created bad blood between us. I wanna do my thing with this new plug over in Buck Town, but Bonkers is looking to corner the market. I need that nigga out of the way, and warring ain't gon' do nothing but slow the money. So I'ma need to come at this from a different angle."

"So what do you need from me?" I wanted to know where he was going with things. I really didn't give a fuck, though. I wasn't willing to work with him under any circumstances. I still envied his bitch ass because my father had given him my birthright of obtaining the Vega throne.

"Honestly, when Bonkers get to sweating Kammron, I just need for you to go at him with all that you got. Try and crush that nigga. He'll be attacked from two different sides, so it should make your job a lot easier. And when Bonkers retreats to go back and reload or to get his shit together out in Brooklyn, that's when me and my army will attack his ass with the hopes of killing him off. Once those niggas are dead, we can take over these boroughs, and then work together to see what we can accomplish."

I laughed. "And the major money thing you were talking about?"

"The Gomez's have been attacked by Vorsky and his men. They are wounded and looking for allies to assist them in their war against the Russians. They are willing to pay up to fifty acres of their heroin fields."

I rubbed my chin. "Fifty acres ain't much, but it's most definitely a start." I nodded. "I'll get to the bottom of that. Why are they coming to us for assistance? Our families have hated each other since the beginning of time."

Tristian shrugged his shoulders. "I don't know, and I don't trust them. The message was relayed to me, and I've done my part by making sure that you've heard it. On another note, have you found out anything in regards to Brittany and her grandparents?"

I sat back on the couch and shook my head. "Nope, and I ain't been looking for no information either, Tristian. I keep telling you that I didn't give a fuck about that li'l girl, nor them old ass people. Whatever happened to them ain't got nothin' to do with me. Let's keep it like that." I got to scratching like crazy. That was the only thing that I hated about being off of those Percocets, them bitches kept you itching, and from time to time, it affected how I enjoyed my high.

Tristian sat across from me staring at the floor with an angry look spread over his face. "You know, from day one we ain't been nothing but a plague to that baby. It ain't her fault that she wanted to go to the park that day to have fun with her friends. She didn't know that you were about to stir up some shit that would cause an all-out shooting war, and she definitely didn't know that she would be hit in the process."

"And what, bruh? My son didn't know that he was about to lose his whole ass life. But he did, and life goes on." I scooted to the edge of the sofa. "As long as a mafucka driving looking into the rear view mirror the whole time, he'll never be able to see where he is going. That goofy mafucka gon' crash into everything. So fuck looking back. It's on my shoulders to restore the Vegas, and for me to get us to where we need to be. Fuck whatever happened in the past because we can't change that shit." I mugged him. "Don't bring yo monka-ass over here ever again talking about no fuckin' Brittany. She ain't my problem. You fuckin' her mother, so that makes her yours. Word the fuck up." I snatched my drink off the table and chugged it down half way.

Tristian sucked his teeth. "I have been looking up to you my whole life, thinking that you are who I should aspire to be like. I always saw how hoes chased you, and how the niggas from Harlem and Havana respected you as a Don. That shit intrigued me, and it made me want to follow behind a street legend like you." He kept looking at the floor for a second until slowly his eyes trailed up to mine. "Until now that is." He started to clench his jaw. "Yo, I know I'm yo li'l brother, but I don't see you in that same light that I used to, Showbiz. Now all I see is the real selfish ass you, and that shit makes me angry that I have been tricked by you all of these years, thinking that you were that deal."

"And so what, Tristian? What are you saying?" I was getting heated. I had a hundred round Draco under the couch and I was ready to pull that bitch out and give him ninety nine of them to the face. The pills had me feening for a kill. I didn't give a fuck if he was my own brother.

"I'ma make this very simple. I still got love for you, Showbiz, because you are my brother. But if I ever find out that you got anything to do with the disappearance of Brittany, there is going to be a major problem between us. That you can bank on." He stood up. "Handle yo bidness wit' these Coke Kings, and I'll do likewise with Bonkers. Later, nigga."

He left out of the den and then the mansion with me doing everything that I could to not murder him in cold blood. Instead, I lay back on the couch with a million thoughts going through my mind of how I was going to restore the Vegas and crush all of our old and new enemies all at once. Now that the Gomezes were under the gun by the same Russians that had dismantled the Vegas, I smelled blood, and it was a must that I went in for the kill, all while capitalizing off of their vulnerabilities.

Chapter 6

Deborah, Tristian's mother, summoned me up to her mansion out in North Carolina two weeks later. She'd just gotten back from Dubai, and she'd said that it was imperative that I meet with her so that we could conduct business that Tristian was giving her a hard time about. I decided that I was going to go and fuck with her right away.

Deborah was a real estate mogul. She had more than twenty million dollars tucked away in the bank, and at least another fifty million tied up in investments and stocks. Whenever she and I got the chance to sit down, I had a habit of leaving with valuable information, and in a stronger position than before I ever got into her presence. So I felt that the meeting was more than necessary.

During this week, Harlem was locked into a deadly civil war against itself. On one side you had Kammron's Coke Kings, and on the other you had my Vega Blood niggas, who were willing to do anything to move up in ranks. I'd put out a decree that for every Coke King they knocked, I would add ten thousand dollars to their end of the week salary. And after they smoked twenty, I would put them in a higher position within our outfit. The higher up you were, the more money you were able to make within the family.

To be honest, it was all psychological. The troops that were on the front lines shooting and killing with reckless abandonment were the ones that were dispensable to me. I didn't give a fuck about them, or their families. The more bodies they dropped, the stronger it made me look as the head. When people in New York and abroad heard the name Showbiz, it struck fear in their hearts. That's what I needed. I needed that fear because, although most times when a man feared you, he came up with a million ways to get rid of you, there were also the times when it made those in fear honor your standing, and they got the fuck out of the way when they saw you coming.

In New York, we didn't give a fuck about a nigga's standing or what he was supposed to have done to somebody over there. We knew that shit wasn't about to happen to us. So it made us go ten times harder. But just like in every city, New York had pussy niggas as well. Before I sent my troops on a rampage against Kammron's, the Vegas were only working with eight blocks. After two months, we had forty blocks, and owned the entire Harlem River Houses. We flushed out other dope boys and sent their crews running for other boroughs. Our standing was getting larger in the game, and it was on me to add to it.

* * *

I rolled up to Deborah's mansion in a cherry red drop-top Ferrari, sitting on red and black rims, with the all-black leather interior that had Showbiz stitched into the headrests. Mecca drove, and I'd laid back in the passenger's seat the whole time. After seeing how she'd gotten down in Washington D.C., I'd decided to make her my long term security, and closest counselor to the streets. She often had real good advice, and refused to hold back any punches with me. I needed that real shit. Nothin' else would suffice.

She pulled into the driveway and threw the car in park. "Say, Biz, how long have you been here talking to Tristian's mother?" The sunlight was shining through the windshield brightly, illuminating her golden face. Her hazel eyes seemed to flicker in the light.

I pulled down the sun visor and glanced over to the all-white mansion that reminded me of the white house. "Shorty always got some major shit she be wanting to politic about, all money, and all advancing. Ain't no telling how long I'm about to be in here."

"Yo, fuck that, then, I'm coming in. I need to make sure that you are straight at all times. I don't know ol' girl, and the way bodies have been dropping, I just don't trust nobody, word up." She reached under her seat and tucked a .45, and then pulled her Nine West blouse back over it. "Let's get it."

I didn't give a fuck. Deborah knew that I was a major nigga and that it was imperative that I kept a shooter with me at all times. So when she opened the door, wearing a purple and black Prada dress that clung to her natural southern curves, with her curly hair hanging over her chest, and both Mecca and I stood before her, all she could do was sigh. "Let me guess, son, this must be one of your gunners?"

"You damn right. Mecca, this is my mother, Deborah. Mama, this is Mecca, my right hand."

Deborah bucked her eyes. "Right hand? Wow, I ain't never heard you use that term for your own brother." She reached out and shook Mecca's hand. "How does a little girl as pretty as you are wind up being a cold hearted drug lord's right hand? You look like you should be somewhere modeling." She eyed the long scar on the side of Mecca's face then looked into her eyes.

"Harlem. Ain't no dreams to be fulfilled in Uptown. I do what it takes. Now, yo' bidness is with him, and not me." She stepped behind me and surveyed the mansion as we stepped inside of it.

It was huge, all white with black leather furniture. The chandeliers looked as if they were made of crystals. The walls held expensive paintings of strong black women like Michelle Obama, Janelle Monèt, Oprah Winfrey, Shonda Rimes, and Angela Bassett, and that was just to name a few. The floors were marble, and the tops as well. They were so shiny that as we walked along them, I could see our reflections in them. She had maids going about the mansion dusting and cleaning. She leaned into me and smiled.

"What you grinning about?" I asked, smelling the Prada perfume coming off of her.

"I didn't think that you were even going to come. Your brother makes it seem as if you are impossible now." She pointed up the spiral of steps. "We'll converse upstairs. Did you know that this used to be Michael Jordan's mansion? His third one to be exact. After visiting here for a few parties, I decided that I wanted it, and well, here we are."

I didn't give a fuck about Jordan. I liked LeBron. Jordan was from Brooklyn, anyway. He wasn't a role model of mine. As far as role models went, I always looked up to Nicky Barnes and Hoffa, dope gods. Fuck everybody else. "Yo, that's what's up."

When we made it to her media room, she stopped and looked over my shoulder at Mecca. "What are you going to do about that?"

Mecca spoke up. "Y'all gon' head and talk business. I'ma keep looking around to make sure that everything is good." She walked away from us.

Deborah stepped into the room, and I entered behind her, watching her ass jiggle as it poked out of her dress. I closed the door behind me. The media room had a big projector and eight movie theater-like seats inside of it. There was also a bar with some of the most expensive champagnes and wines. I wasn't focused on any of that. As soon as that door closed, I had my arms wrapped around Deborah's waist and was humping my front into her juicy ass, while I sucked on her neck.

"Un-uh, Showbiz. Don't start this shit. Mama ain't call you over here for that. You said you weren't gon' come at me like that no more."

I turned her around until her forehead was against mine. My hands roamed all over her ass. Deborah was thick as hell, and so bad, even though she was in her upper forties. She was the sole reason why I had a lustful thing for older women. To this day, I still think that older women are the sexiest women on earth, especially the ones that kept themselves up like she did.

I sucked on her neck. "Mama, I want some of you." My hands caused the Prada dress to rise. Her naked ass cheeks came on display. I rubbed the hot skin, and licked all over her neck, and then bit her hard.

"Unnnnn, shit. I'm your brother's mother. I damn near raised you, baby. You gotta stop this. It's not right." She tried to push herself away from me.

My hand dipped into her thong from the back, went into her crotch, and cupped her naked pussy. It felt freshly waxed. The lips were juicy, and slightly parted. I dropped to my knees and pushed her over the bar, spaced her thighs, and licked up each one. "You my mama. If I wanna eat this pussy, that's what I'ma do. You shouldn't be so mafuckin' fine."

My tongue traveled up her legs and stopped at her crease. I sucked her pussy lips, opened them, and slipped my tongue as deep inside of her as I could, before pulling it out and licking circles around her pearl tongue. The clitoris popped out. I trapped it with my lips and then sucked on it. She beat her fist on the bar and pushed a bottle of white wine out of the way.

"Uhhhhh, Showbiz, you dirty little boy. You so fuckin' nasty. Shit." She hit the bar with her fist again.

I slurped all over her pussy while I held the lips wide open, manipulating her clit until she shivered and moaned loudly, cumming all over my face. Her cream oozed down my throat, and I swallowed as much as I could before standing up.

just her bra and panties. Her camel toe was always visible, and her nipples were hard. She was super lovey dovey and never had a problem with my wandering hands.

Her pussy gripped me. Her juices dripped off of my sack and slid down my thighs. We kissed passionately. Her tongue licked my face and then she bit my neck so hard that it made me fuck her faster and deeper. We fell to the floor with me pounding her out like I had something to prove. Her pussy got better and better. I started whimpering because it was that good. I came. She screamed while biting me and came hard. We rolled over, she arched her back and rode me as only a vet could. Her hand was around my neck, choking me as best she could, while she bounced up and down with me feeling all over her titties. She laid her cheek against mine. "You're my son, and you're fuckin' me. Yo daddy would kill us both. If Tristian ever found out, he would... Uhhhhhhh shit," she screamed as she fucked me harder.

I held her ass. "Tristian wishes he could hit this pussy."

She buckled. "Shut up. Shut up." She rode me faster.

"If he could fuck you, he would go crazy. Ain't nobody pussy as good as yours, mama. Fuck me like I'm him. Fuck yo baby."

She whimpered and closed her eyes tight. She was fucking me so fast that I had to hold on to her waist. I yanked her dress all the way off of her shoulders so that her brown titties could jump up and down. Her nipples were longer than I had ever seen them before. She groaned and opened her mouth wide.

"I'm gonna cum. I'm finna cum, baby. Uhhh shittttttt." She rotated her hips at full speed and shuddered, falling on top of me. Her pussy gripped me off and on, like a tight fist. She oozed all over me and slowly worked her cat. Her tongue licked all over my neck. I was cumming in her again. She

T.J. Edwards

milked me slowly now. I could smell our combined scents. It drove me crazy.

"Mmm, you so nasty, Showbiz. Why would you make me think of some sick stuff like that?" She popped my chest.

"Y'all sexy ass mothers don't know what y'all be doing to us li'l niggas. We are looking, and we can't help how that shit affects us. You bad, Deborah. Ain't no way we could've really been kin because I don't know if I would've been able to be in the house with you alone."

"You're just saying that because I really ain't your biological mother. If I was, I'm sure that you would've never looked at me the way that you do now."

I stood up and got myself together as best I could. I knew that I was going to need a shower real soon. I didn't like the stench of sex on me. "Yo, I'm finna get in this water and when I come out, I want you to break everything down to me. Cool?"

She stepped into my face, pulling her Prada dress back over her thighs. I saw that my semen was leaking down her legs before she covered them back up. She leaned into my face. "That sounds good, baby. You go and do that. I gotta catch one, too, and then try to see if I can find out where this little girl wandered off to." She kissed my lips ever so lightly, while holding the back of my head. When she broke the kiss, she had a smile on her face. "Thank God, you really didn't come from me. I would've been in trouble."

I couldn't do anything but laugh at that. I left out of the room and hopped in the shower, after treating my nose to a bit of luxury dog food. I wondered what Deborah was up to.

Chapter 7

I sat in front of the projector screen while Deborah stood to the side of it with a pointer stick in her hand. On the end of the stick was a laser that made it easier for her to show me what she was trying to get me to understand about a certain area of the screen.

"So anyway, as I was saying, since you and your army are bigger and stronger than Tristian's, I thought it was time to drop this in your lap. Firstly, you have my condolences for the many Vega lives lost during the war against the Russians. I wish I could've been able to do something to prevent it from happening, but as you already know, your family didn't think too highly of me because of the color of my skin, and my roots originating in Grenada.

"You see, before I ever met Chico Vega, our grandparents were at war within the sugar industry. Your father's people had about two hundred acres of sugarcane back then, while mine had just a hundred acres of sugarcane, but three hundred acres of Tobacco. Long story short, after the Great Depression, times were hard and both of our families were looking for a way to make ends meet. The only viable option seemed to be to turn to narcotics, since drugs were all the craze of many depressed people, due to job loss, marriages that ended, and overall so many lost and displaced people. They needed an escape.

"My grandfather turned all three hundred acres of our to-bacco into coke fields. We started to super grow plants that would help us to be able to produce the richest cocaine in all of Grenada. Within ten years' time, our family took off. And with a few conscious plugs, we were able to sew up the is-lands, before venturing over to the Midwest of the United

States, which was easier to break into than New York back in those days.

"The Vegas followed suit only a year after we did, and then the Gomezes. After a while, our families became drug empires and we were able to supply nearly the entire United States, with some interruption from other drug families. Anyway, the reason I am bringing this to your attention is because, although the Vegas may have never liked me, I have always loved you and Miguel, and my son will forever be a Vega. However, Tristian, is unwilling to seek retribution for the Vegas, but I know that you are. I have a sure way for you to seek retribution, all the while crushing the Gomezes, and Vorsky. It is risky, but it will prove to be effective. In addition to crushing these foes, you will be able to take over everything that the Gomezes have built, as well as recover all that the Putin's have conquered on the islands.

"If you follow my playbook to the tee, not only will you go down as the greatest Vega to ever live, but you will be filthy rich, and will have fully restored your people. And it all starts with this man right here." She placed the laser on the face of a golden colored Arab looking man. He had a white thing on his head, and was sitting in a big chair that was made of gold. Beside him were two scantily clad women with big leaves in their hands. They waved the leaves up and down to keep him cool. It was clear that he was sitting inside of a grand palace. His neck was flooded with gold, and he had a big diamond on each finger.

"Yo, who is that nigga right there?"

"His name is Khabir Aziz. He is a Saudi Prince, and many of the men that were linked to the Nine Eleven attacks were reported to have come from under his regime. While none of it has ever been proven, he has a history of being remorselessly deadly."

"Okay, so what does he have to do with me?" I drank from the fresh squeezed orange juice that her maid had supplied me with.

"Khabir is fresh to the throne of the Aziz's, and he has a strong hatred for the United States of America. Due to the fact that he is forbidden from stepping foot on this land, he has tried desperately to find an animal like himself that leads a crew of money hungry savages for the purposes of getting filthy rich beyond your imagination through channels of narcotics, trade, wall street, real estate, and of course, the slums. All areas of the game that, with my help, you will be able to succeed greatly in."

I rubbed my chin hairs again. "Yo, kid look like he gon' be damn near impossible to touch bases with. On top of that, you know like I know that time is money. What would inspire this man to have a sit down with me? What is his method of income right now?"

"The meeting will be because of me." She smiled solicitously. "And as far as his hustle goes, he has his hands into everything, but the Aziz family generates billions of dollars a year through their tech and energy investments. All extremely lucrative stocks that are also within your scope to acquire through my guidance."

"Awright, so what's his agenda? Let's say I go over here and meet with him? What is he going to want?"

"First, he will have you crush the Gomezes. Secondly, he will give you the Holy Grail to eradicating the Russians and taking over the land that they have stolen from your family, and other islanders. Lastly, he will use you to penetrate the drug market in North America like never before. You will completely dominate the game, and the Vegas will once again be held in the highest esteems, but only this time it will not be Chico Vega as the king, but you, Juanito."

I sat up, imagining the possibilities. "Yo, I like the sound of that."

She laughed. "I know you do. Now the first step is to set up the meeting. I'll pull a few strings through a few different channels that will ultimately make it up to Khabir. Expect to take flight in two weeks. As you say, time is money, and for you there are millions to be made."

I stood up and pulled her to me, cuffing that fat ass booty. "And for you?"

"The same. I would never set things up the way that I am unless I had a hidden agenda. Besides, I've always been involved with kings. Why should I switch it up now?" She slipped her hand into my pants and cuffed my dick. "We have to invest in the pharmaceutical companies as much as possible right now. I had word from an insider that they are about to amplify this COVID-19 pandemic. Everybody is going to go running to buy pills that are designed to boost their immune systems. It'll be a cash cow. The pharmaceutical industry will beat this virus for all it's worth, and then they will present the public with a cure that they've had all along. Trust me, I know what I'm talking about. It's all about money. Are you with me?"

"Hell yeah, how much do you need from me?" I had no idea how the stock market worked, but Deborah was saying all of the things that made sense to me. She spoke like she really knew what she was talking about. Since she had so much money, I had to give her the benefit of the doubt.

She sucked my bottom lip into her mouth again. "For your willingness to follow my lead, I will invest a million dollars in your name. We'll split the return. How does that sound?"

I picked her up and she wrapped her thighs around me. "Sounds like I'm finna spend the night tonight and wear yo ass out."

She snickered. "Ain't nobody scared of you. I'm yo mama." She held my head while I tongued her ass down.

***

That night, I stood in the mirror re-braiding the ends of my hair. Mecca sat on the bed with her thick thighs crossed. Her head was turned sideways. "Yo, Showbiz, let me ask you somethin', kid, and you ain't gotta answer the question if you don't want to."

"Aiight, shoot." I kept doing my thing while Li'l Baby's 'My Turn' album banged through the speakers of the room.

"You grew up with Tristian right?"

"Yeah, that's my li'l brother. Of course, I did."

"I'm talkin' in the same house? You called his mother, mama, too, right?"

"Always had and always will. Why, what you getting at?"

Mecca slid off of the bed. Her short Fendi dressed raised on her thighs and flashed me her pink panties. The crotch looked fat. She was thick as a muthafucka. Keeping my hands to myself was becoming harder and harder. She stepped beside me. "Say, Dunn, how can you fuck your brother's mother?"

I froze for a second, and looked over at her. "That's what you wanted to ask me?"

She nodded. "Yeah. I heard you in there giving her ass the bidness. I mean, it wasn't like she was trying to keep that shit a secret. She was moaning and groaning loud as hell. But still, how could you?"

I laughed. "That's a bad bitch in there, Mecca. She got millions, she got flavor, and I grew up lusting over her."

"But still, she had a baby with your father, and that baby is Tristian. You didn't feel no type of way while you were fuckin' her?"

"Other than happy, nall. I don't give no fuck about Tristian, or my pops. Pussy is pussy. It is what it is."

She scooted down the dresser until she was standing in my face. "That's how you really feel?"

"About what?"

"You just said that pussy was pussy. That means that it doesn't matter to you. What about me?" Her hazel eyes beamed into mine.

I felt a way right away. "What about you?"

"I've been rockin' wit' you for a minute now. You ain't never made a move on me. What's the reason for that? Is it cause I act too hood?"

"What? Hell nall. You bugging, shorty. Get yo ass out of my way." I tried to move her, but she stayed in place.

"Nall, not until we get to the bottom of this. Is it because I got this scar going down the right side of my face? Do you find me ugly?" Now her nose was almost touching mine.

"Shorty, you one of the baddest bitches I've ever seen in my life. That scar only adds to your beauty, for me."

"Then what is it? Is it the way my crib was? Or maybe because my mother is a hype."

"Yo, most of the parents in Harlem are rolling off of something. That shit can't be held against you, or nobody else, other than that parent."

"Is it my age? What? You think that if we go there that I'ma tell on you or somethin'?"

"I ain't worried about that snitch shit coming from you."

She stepped on her tippy toes and kissed me. "I'm horny. I want you to fuck me like you just did that lady in there. I don't know if I can take it, seeing as I ain't never been with no grown nigga before, but I'm willing to try as long as you the grown nigga that's on top of me. I want you to see me with lust and desire. I know I may be a killa and all that, but I still got that womanly side of me that needs to be fulfilled. Plus, I'm loyal to just you. I'd kill another man in a heartbeat. I wanna kill that old lady in there because you just fucked her. but how can I blame you when you and I ain't even doing nothing?" She rubbed my chest with her hands, avoiding my eyes. "I want you. I'm ready. Please."

I moved her hands off of me, and stepped out of her face. "Yo, I ain't trying to go there with you, Mecca. I got crazy love for you. I don't know how that shit gon' change once my dick goes in you. So why risk it?"

She nodded. "I said what I said, and you know how I feel. It's out there. I'ma fall back, and play my role, though. Good night." She climbed onto the bed with her skirt up her thighs. They jiggled along with her ass.

She looked so good. I wanted to go there with her so bad, but I knew how I was when it came to pussy. Once I had a woman, she more often than not became old news to me, and I didn't want that to happen to Mecca. I looked at her almost like a little cousin that was crazy about me, and I her. I knew that she was going to be in my circle, and at my right hand, for a long time, and I didn't want to jeopardize our relationship.

"Say, Goddess, I don't want you thinking that I ain't trying to go there with you because there is somethin' wrong with you, because it ain't. I'm just terrible when it comes to men and women type relationships. Yo, I'ma dog, hand to God. But on some real shit, when you climbed in the bed just then, and I was able to see a hint of those thighs, and earlier I saw ya panties, word to Harlem, I thought about what it would feel like to sink ten inches deep in that li'l pussy. I'm just scared of what's gon' happen after I do." I sat on the bed next to her, and looked her body over lustfully.

She laid back with the hem of the skirt just below the top of her thighs. They were golden brown and plump. Her knees looked darker, and for some reason, that was even sexy to me. She ran her hand over her stomach.

"Yo, you know how many niggas in Harlem be having li'l young broads like me ducked off? This shit is normal where we from. I don't know a chick my age in the projects that's messing with a broke li'l dude her age. What can they offer us? A few pumps and then it's all over." She slid her hand down, and slowly pulled up the hem of her skirt. Her pink tongue cruised over her lips. "Showbiz, I think you're scared of this young pussy. You too accustomed to fuckin' them old broads." She slowly opened her thighs. The skirt wound up around her waist. The lower portion of her belly was on display. Her fingers rubbed the front of her panties. "What's it gon' take for you to fuck me right here and right now?"

Chapter 8

I walked across the bed until I was beside her. My hand rubbed up her thighs, I moved them apart and stuck my nose right on the middle of her underwear. I sniffed hard, and licked the front of them. She moaned, and arched her back.

"Be careful with me. I might be on that killa shit for you, but I'm normal. I'm just a girl. I'm fragile, Showbiz."

The more she talked, the more excited I became. Her li'l coochie smelled fresh through the panties. The lips were molded to the fabric. I knew before I even pulled the panties down that she was strapped under there. When I slid them down her thighs, she opened her legs all the way. Her golden sex lips were bald and pudgy, and already wet. Her clitoris peeked out of the hood. The nipples on her chest were rock hard. I kissed all over both of her calve muscles. Then I trailed my tongue all the way up until I was licking right over her folds. She reached in between her legs, and opened them to show me her pink. Her cream seeped out of her middle. I sniffed her box again until my nose was wet.

"Li'l mama, I wanna eat this li'l pussy. You about to make me do some shit to yo li'l ass that I never thought I would do before. You fuckin' up my head. I'ma give you one more chance. Get yo ass up and go sleep in the other room."

"No, I want you. I'ma rider for you. I've killed for you. You're all the fuck I see. Now fuck me. I earned it." She rubbed her middle finger around her clitoris over and over until she was whimpering and bucking her hips forward. Her mouth opened wide. "Showbiz, please, I'm on fire right now."

I was shaking. The chains around my neck were rubbing against the sheets on the bed. I snuck between her thick thighs and kissed her coochie. She moaned. I kissed it again, but this time, I swiped at the hood and her clit. She rested her fingers on top of my braids, and forced me further into her middle. I threw caution to the wind. There wasn't anything like new pussy. I couldn't help myself, no matter how hard I tried. I separated her folds with my thumbs and opened her up, before my tongue went to work like a savage.

She threw her ankles around my neck and moaned loudly. "Showbiz. Showbiz. Showbiz. Unh. Unh. My God."

I pushed her knees to her chest and got gross while I ate that pussy. I rubbed my face all in it, nose and everything. The louder she moaned, the more it encouraged me to go harder. Before the five minute mark, she was stuffing my face into her gap and cumming while screaming at the top of her lungs. Her ankles beat on my back. I sucked both sex lips at the same time, and drank her juices. After she came the second time, she pushed me away, shaking as if she were outside in the freezing cold.

"Damn, Biz, what did you just do to me." She scooted, all the way back to the headboard, rubbing her gap. The juices wet her fingers.

I wiped my mouth. "That's that grown man shit, shorty. That's what I'm telling you. You ain't ready for a nigga like me. Word up." I got out of the bed and walked to the bedroom door, ready to go out of it so I could track down Deborah and tear her ass up. Mecca had me feeling like I needed to relieve myself in the worst way.

She jumped out of the bed and nearly broke her neck to get to the door. Once there, she dropped down to her knees. "I might not be ready for the dick yet, but you gon' at least let me show you my gratitude. She rubbed my pants front. Let me see it."

I was throbbing. My dick was sticking up against my Fendi shorts. She cupped upward and squeezed it. I moved her hand away. "Gon', li'l baby. I'm trying as hard as I can to not smash yo ass. You making it real hard."

She squeezed me. "Fuck what you talkin' bout, I wanna see. What, you want me to beg or somethin'?" She looked up at me with her hazel eyes. "Please, Biz. Please let me see it." She batted her eyelashes and sucked her bottom lip, looking fine as hell.

I didn't even stop her when she unbuckled my Ferragamo belt, and pulled my piece right out of my Fendi boxers. Her eyes got bucked. She tried to pump it with her left hand and switched to her right. The entire time she stared at it as if she couldn't believe that she had it in her hand. She pulled it down and kissed it softly.

"I changed my mind. I want you to do it to me." She stood up and scooted back to the bed with her hand still wrapped around my pole. She sat on the bed, pumping it. She pulled the skin back, and sucked me into her mouth, only about four inches. Her lips moved up and down it lovely. She slurped loudly, and moaned all around it. My hand slipped between her thick thighs. I found her pussy oozing. She panted, and scooted forward into my hand.

She popped me out of her mouth for a moment. "I want you, Showbiz. Ain't no man ever cared about me before. I know you care about me because you ain't never tried to go in on me. All dem niggas in our borough used to try and pay my mother to fuck me, but they never got that chance. I ain't have no problem dropping they ass when I caught them slipping, word up. But I want you. I need you. I need that boss shit in me."

She sucked me back in and went to work like a professional. Her head moved back and forward at full speed, while her breasts bounced on her chest. She groaned while my fingers dove deep. I sped up the pace and got to finger fucking her so fast that I began to sweat. She opened her knees, and arched her back again. Her face remained in my lap. My thumb ran circles around her clitoris. She bucked, popped me out of her mouth again, and came, moaning at the top of her lungs. Her pussy squirted jets of her juices at me.

I'd had all I could take. I picked her little ass up and tossed her back on the bed, dropped my shorts and climbed between her thighs. I lined myself up, and rubbed the head up and down her slit before slipping into her, balls deep.

"Unnnn!" Her eyes closed tightly. She wrapped her ankles around my waist and pulled me into her. "Shit, Showbiz, it hurt a little. Wait a minute. Please." She wiggled from side to side. Her nails dug into my shoulders.

I leaned into her face. "Where you from, Goddess?"

"Harlem. Born and bred." She gasped as if she was out of breath. Her mouth hung wide open.

I licked all over her lips. "Then why the fuck you asking me to take it easy on you? I thought that killa shit was in your heart?"

"It is, Showbiz. You know it is." She scooted backward a bit to ease some of my dick out of her.

I grabbed her to me, and kissed all over her scar that ran the length of the right side of her face. "I think you're gorgeous, Goddess. Word up. Harlem breed Queens, ma, and you are most definitely that."

I cocked back and slammed into her. She yelped and held me tighter. I did it again. Her teeth bit into my neck. Then I was fucking her like she was supposed to be fucked. Long strokes, back to back. Pulling her to me while I dug deep inside of her womb.

"Unnn. Unnn. Showbiz. You fucking me. You finally fucking me. Unnn shit." She fell back, and allowed for me to pound her out while she whimpered and moaned.

86

Her pussy was tight, and she was most certainly a virgin. I felt the tear of her secret place. That only caused me to really give her the bidness, though. The first time meant that I couldn't take it easy on her. It meant that she would remember it for the rest of her life. I was that one for her. I plunged and plunged, sucking all over her neck, digging into her guts.

"Unh. Unh. Unh. I got you, Mecca." More plunging. Deep strokes. Her thighs opened up further. "Word to Harlem, I got you for as long as I'm king." I licked her scar again, and proceeded to roll my back.

She sat up and licked all over my chest. She bit into it, and fell back, squeezing her titties. She pulled her shoulder straps down to free them. Her nipples were thick and long as the tips on a baby's bottle.

"Showbiz, I can't handle it. I can't handle it. It's too deep. It's too deep." She tried to push me away. I slammed home and came deep in her pussy. At the same time, she came all over me. She shivered and I groaned loudly in her ear, licking it. I fell on top of her, still slowly stroking. She was so wet that the slouching was loud in the room. Finally, I stopped, and rolled on my side. She rolled with me, and hugged up to me.

"Please don't pull out, not yet, not yet."

I rolled onto my back with her laying on top of me. We were still connected. She laid on my chest and slowly worked her hips until I was rock hard again. She sat up and rode me slow. Her perfect titties danced in the dim light. She looked into my eyes. "Yo, I'd never switch sides on you, Showbiz. I'm Vega crazy, word up. I'm riding with you until they take the air out of my lungs. I don't care where you are, or where you go, as long as I am right there with you." She kissed my lips and slowly rode me until she came again, then she collapsed on my chest and stayed there.

***

That night, we lay naked, cuddled up in the bed with me behind her. "Showbiz, I hope you don't think that this is going to stop me from handling my business for you as your top security, because it ain't. I just couldn't see no other nigga ever going in my body. It had to be you. You own me." She closed her eyes and pulled my right arm until it was around her.

I kissed the back of her head. "What's understood need not be explained. Get some sleep, li'l baby. I ain't going nowhere. Word up." She rolled around and we hugged up. She opened her eyes for a second to peek at me, and then closed her eyes back. Even though I wasn't with all that cuddling shit, Mecca was my baby, and it felt good to make an exception for her. Besides, she'd earned her stripes in the field, and I knew that she was cut from the same cloth as me.

Chapter 9

Dubai, United Arab Emirates

Three weeks later, I took a first class flight to Dubai, United Arab Emirates to meet up with Khabir Aziz. After Deborah, Kalani, Mecca, and myself made it back to Hotel Jumeirah, and got all of our things put away, Kalani wasn't able to sit still. She wanted to hit up the city right away on some tourist type shit. I stood there in the full length mirror, looking over my Prada short set. I added three gold ropes, and slipped a gold diamond faced Patek Philippe on to my left wrist, and a gold iced Richard Mille on my right one. The two carat diamonds in my ear lobes offset my ensemble. Kalani had braided my hair straight to the back. She put the beads on my tips to match my fit. Lastly, I slipped into a pair of Balenciaga runners, and I was good to go. I was feeling stellar, and ready to get plugged in with Khabir, until Kalani kept on getting on my damn nerves.

"Daddy, we gotta see what that beach down there is like. I ain't never seen a beach where there is really white sand. Damn, we came up in the world." She smiled and fit her last diamond into her right ear lobe. She sort of nudged me to the side so she could look over her Burberry skirt dress that fit her like a second skin. Her ass was poked out further than I remembered, and she smelled good. She kissed my cheek. "Yo, I swear I should've chosen you from the beginning. Ain't no nigga in New York getting money like you, Showbiz. Word up, you getting crazy dollars. I'm close to saying fuck Brooklyn."

I laughed at that. "Shorty, you too much. Yo li'l ratchet ass just ain't never been out of New York before. Now that you chilling on a whole other continent, you feel like this shit is major. What you are failing to realize is that this is a business trip. The reason I am here is so I can further my hustle. All that kicking it and other shit come last. Now I brought you with me because I thought you were going to be able to handle this. But if you ain't, then I'm 'bout to put yo' ass on a coach flight back to New York."

"Coach?" She scrunched her face. "Yeah right, I ain't even about to accept a coach purse from you. Fuck I look like riding in coach when my nigga running New York? Check yo self, daddy? Straight up." She rolled her eyes. "But it's good, though. If you want me to fall back while you go off and do your thing, I'm cool with that. Just tell me what you want me to do."

There were three knocks at the front door of our Presidential suite. Mecca, who was standing looking out of the window, on security, gripped her Glock that had been provided in the limo that Deborah had waiting for us, along with a few other weapons. Mecca made her way to the door and looked out of the peephole. "It's Deborah. What you want me to do?"

"Let her in." I turned to Kalani. "Yo, for now, you gon' chill ya ass up here until I find out what the program is going to be. You understand me?"

She turned away from me and walked off. She took her ear buds and placed them in her ears while she listened to music, glaring at me. "Whatever."

Mecca and I made eye contact. She broke it right away, and looked off. I met Deborah halfway to the door. She waved me over. When I got to her, she stepped into my face and looked up at me.

"Listen, Khabir will be flying back into Dubai from China tomorrow evening. We will meet him at his palace then. He's sending a chopper. Until then, if you want to enjoy the city, that will be just fine. I have other pressing matters to attend to, and then both you and I can meet up later for a night cap. That's if you will be able to free yourself from these two." She said all of these things low enough for only me to hear her. Though by the expression on Mecca's face, I could tell that she was able to hear her as well.

"That sounds good. What time is the best time for you?"

"Ten o'clock. My suite. There is a nightly view that will blow your mind. I look forward to seeing you then. Until then, you are more than free to use the yacht. Here's my card, and pass. They'll be expecting you, son." She winked at me, and then kissed me on both cheeks and walked away with her ass jiggling under her blue and gold Versace dress. I tucked the card into my pocket.

Mecca closed the door behind her. "Everything cool, Showbiz?"

I nodded. "But let me holla at you in the bathroom real quick. She nodded and went in first. Before I followed her, I stopped and looked over to Kalani. She was lying flat out on her back with her ear buds still in her ears. I waved my hand. She sat up. "Get yo li'l stubborn ass up and get ready. We about to hit up Dubai."

She screeched and jumped up. She rushed to her makeup lot and got to getting ready. "I can't wait. I ain't never been here before."

I stepped into the bathroom, and closed the door behind me. Mecca stood with her back against the wall. I grabbed her and pulled her to me. My lips were all over hers. My hands cuffed her fat ass booty, and then I was sucking all over her neck. She moaned. I tongued her down for two full minutes, and left her breathing hard with her nipples poking up against her blouse.

"What was that for?" She asked with her voice raspy.

"I just been thinking about you. I know we on bidness right now, but you still got my black heart. I fucks wit' you, you understand me."

She nodded. She poked my chest. "Say, kid, I respect you, but that bitch out there act more immature than me, and she gotta be five years older than me. I ain't feeling her, but I ain't about to get on no jealous shit either. You do you, but just know that I said what I said."

I looked her over. "You getting jealous on me, killa?"

"What? Nigga, never that. I'm just stating the obvious. I don't care what you do." She held my gaze for a minute, then looked off. "Okay, maybe a little. But girls get like that when they lose their virginity to a boy. In this case, I lost mine to a grown ass man. Can you blame me for feeling how I'm feeling?"

"Hell yeah, I can." I snatched the gun off of her waist and pressed it to her forehead. I cocked the hammer. "Bitch, you getting soft on me?"

She frowned. "Hell nall."

"You letting my dick control yo' punk ass emotions? Huh?" I pressed the gun harder into her forehead.

"N'all, Biz, damn." Her eyes watered.

"Kid, what is this? Huh, what is this?"

She swallowed the lump in her throat. "This is Harlem."

"This what?"

"This is Harlem." She wiped her tears away. "This is Harlem. This is Harlem. This is Harlem," she hollered. More tears fell. "This is Harlem."

I took the gun off of her and pulled her into my arms. "Damn, baby, I told you we shouldn't have crossed over like that. You're just a girl trying to be a woman." I hugged her tighter.

"What is it about Kalani that you like so much? What does she have that I don't?"

I hugged her closer to me and kissed her lips. "Nothing. You my mafuckin' li'l baby. Ain't no baby like my baby. She just got here first, but you come from the gutter just like me. We from Harlem, the fire pit of New York. I tucked the gun back into her waist, and held her face with both hands. I kissed her.

"I need you to be strong right now. We on a mission. When it's all said and done, it's gon' be me and you. That's my word. Mark that shit in blood."

"Okay." She nodded. She wrapped her arms around my neck. "Thank you, Biz. That's why I'm so loyal to you." She took a step back and looked up at me. "I'm ready to do what needs to be done, now. It's good."

"Cool, and yo, I got love for you right here. Only you. You from the trenches like me. I don't love no mafucka but you. You hear me?"

"Yeah, I hear you, and I love you, too. Right here." She pointed to her chest. And my love for her went up a few more notches.

***

I watched Kalani's perfect toes dig into the white sand while we strolled down the beach. She had white tips on each of them, and they looked so good to me. I've always had a thing for women that kept their toes done properly. The ocean splayed a short distance away from us, and the entire beach was cluttered with people tanning, swimming, chasing one another, or simply walking like her and I were. It was ridiculously hot, with a gentle breeze that needed to step its game up.

T.J. Edwards

"Daddy, what did you have to talk to Mecca about when you pulled her into the bathroom? Was it business?"

I kept walking. I looked over my shoulder. Mecca strolled behind at a safe distance, scanning the beach for potential threats. Even though she was young, she was good at her job. "Don't worry about it. That shit didn't concern you."

"You fuckin' her li'l ass?" She looked up to me and the wind blew her curly hair so that it wound up in her face. Her yellow skin had darkened. She was Puerto Rican and black, but this day she looked more black because the sun had baked her to a darker complexion. She looked good.

"Yep. That's my li'l baby. You know I'm fuckin'."

Kalani stopped and looked over her shoulder at Mecca. Then she looked back at me. "Don't play wit' me, Showbiz. I know you ain't really fuckin' that girl, or calling her your li'l baby, when I'm yo only mafuckin' baby."

"Kalani, if you ask me stupid questions, I'ma give you stupid answers. She got a job to do, and she does her shit real well. Don't worry about my relationship with her, as long as it ain't affecting mine with you. Stay in yo lane before I drop you off."

She sucked her teeth. "The day you drop me off is the day that we both kick the bucket. Nigga, I ain't playing about you. You think I'm about to go and allow you to live your life, when I know from here on out that it is going to be in luxury? Yeah the fuck right. I gotta be a part of all of this shit. You said you had me. Having me doesn't mean kicking me to the curb. Get yo' mind right, Showbiz. Ain't shit sweet wit' me." Her long hair blew in the wind. "All you gotta tell me is if this bitch is a threat to me?"

I glared at her. "Kalani, shut up before I choke yo' ass out, word up. Keep getting on my mafuckin' nerves and I'm sending you back to New York. Now, keep fuckin' wit me."

94

"Dang, calm down. It ain't even that serious." She rolled her eyes. She looked back over her shoulder again. "She's cute and kinda strapped, but she ain't got shit on me, no way. What happened to her face?"

I shook my head. "Yo, don't worry about it. Let's just enjoy the sun and you focus on this shopping spree I'm bout to take yo li'l punk ass on."

"You can call me whatever you wanna call me. Long as you call me fresh, and spoiled." She stuck her tongue out at me and walked ahead so I could watch her ass shake inside of the little thong that she wore down the crack of her backside. It wasn't visible.

The cheeks were kissed by the sun and she was killing shit. There were plenty of East Indian women walking around half naked, and Kalani was crushing all of those broads with no effort. I think I accepted so much from her because she was so bad, and still had come from a shady deal. At one point in time, she'd dated Tristian, and he'd been ready to marry her. I took pleasure in defiling her every time we fucked, just to one up that nigga. I still couldn't believe that my father had handed him my birthright. I would forever be jaded by that fact.

***

That night, Deborah was stuck, and called away on business. But I made it seem to Kalani that I still had to go out and handle some street business, along with Mecca. She was cool with it, after I'd spent fifty thousand dollars on her, shopping on Dubai's version of Rodeo Drive. Sitting back at the hotel, trying on her outfits made her happy, and me as well. Both Mecca and I wound up on the Yacht, standing on the bay, while the boat floated up and down. We were looking up at the stars with me standing behind her. I rested my lips on her neck while I inhaled her scent. "Yo, I love you li'l baby."

She trembled. "I love you, too. And I love when you're all over me like this. It makes me feel so secure." She turned her head sideways and kissed my lips passionately. Then she smiled. "Showbiz, I know you ain't with all of that weak shit, but I just wanted to let you know that you make me feel so happy all the time. I am thankful that you came into my life, and I appreciate everything that you do for me, and for Harlem. That's why I ride for."

I held her more firm. "I do what I'm supposed to do. I got our borough, and us, on my back." I kissed her cheek again. "You my li'l mamas. I'll kill a mafucka over you. This is us. Feel that."

She turned all the way until she was facing me. Her arms wrapped around my neck. "You make me feel like I ain't never felt before. I both love and hate the feeling. I don't like being so vulnerable, but I trust you. Just be careful with me. Please." She laid her head on my chest, and closed her eyes.

I held her in silence. I didn't understand how it was happening, and I didn't even think that it was cool for me to, but I had to admit that I was falling for her out of need for the kind of love that she had deep within her. I didn't care about her money. I didn't care about her status, or where she'd come from. I didn't care about the scar going down the side of her face. All I cared about was her and her heart. That heart that could be cold when the time was right, and warm for me at all times. Mecca was my baby, and I felt a serious way about her.

Chapter 10

Khabir Aziz was a five feet eight inch, golden colored, green eyed Arab, with wavy hair, and a big nose. A day after I spent time with Mecca on Deborah's Yacht, Khabir called for a helicopter to pick up me and Deborah. He didn't allow Mecca nor Kalani to come because this was scheduled to be a private affair. He'd let it be known that I was to be searched at the door of his palace for any weapons or firearms, and I was okay with that. The same went for Deborah.

When we hopped out of the chopper we were led to a Mercedes Benz limousine. Inside was all cherry leather interiors, with a chandelier, and a bucket of Moët. The console was full of cigars fully stuffed with weed, and there was even a place in the console for a bunch of pink Mollie and Oxycontin pills. I didn't touch any of that shit because I hadn't seen the blunts rolled, and I had my own pills.

I was going pretty heavy on the Percs because I was trying the best that I could to kick the heroin habit. It had been two months and I was down to snorting only a few lines a week to keep the sick feeling off of me, even though I was still going through a series of other withdrawal symptoms.

When we pulled up in front of his four story golden palace, there were four armed Arab guards standing in front of the gate. They made us get out and they searched the limo from top to bottom. Then they searched us. After we went through that process, we got back into the limo, went through the gate after it slid to the side to allow our entrance, and then we pulled in front of the palace. We got out and two more guards searched us again, and waved a wand over our bodies.

We were led inside of the palace. As soon as we walked through the door, we were forced to walk slowly through an x-ray machine. Then we were searched again, and walked into the foyer. Khabir met us in the middle of the palace with his hand outstretched. "You must be Showbiz Vega. What a pleasure it is to meet you."

His hands felt too soft. I shook his hand briefly and dropped it. I wasn't with all that touching shit. "The one and only." I watched him hug Deborah. "Yo, I was searched so many times trying to get to come and see you that I feel like I need a bath."

He laughed. "Well, I am a very important man. The Aziz family has many enemies. I must be careful at all times. Please, follow me." He walked off with his red, black, and gold silk Roberto Cavili short and shirt fit waving slightly like a flag in the wind.

Through the windows I could see two full court basketball areas. There was a tennis court, a volleyball court, a golf portion, and there were two scantily clad females riding on the backs of white tigers as if it was the most normal thing in the world.

We wound up in the portion of the mansion where there were all glass windows. There was a clear view of a big body of light blue water, and white sand. We were on the third floor, and directly below us I could also see a big Olympic sized swimming pool in his backyard. The smell of chlorine was prominent. I was mesmerized. I decided right then that my goal was to acquire a palace. Mansions were for low budget ballers. In order to make a statement to the world that you were doing anything, you needed to be living in the same kind of space that Khabir was. We sat in big leather chairs that began to conform to my body as soon as I sat down. I liked that.

An East Indian maid came into the room with a small tablet. "Can I take your order, Mr. Vega?"

I looked over at Khabir. He shrugged his shoulders. "You can order anything you want, even a virgin, if you so please.

98

Age is not an issue. We have all ages and kinds." He sipped from his golden chalice that was encrusted with yellow diamonds.

"Yo, I'm good. I just wanna get down to the nitty gritty," I returned, looking the maid up and down. She was gorgeous.

"If you like her, she is also on the menu. Seventeen, pure Brazilian, a magnificent lover." He winked at her.

I shook my head. Mecca came across my mind. I wondered what she was up to. I prayed that Kalani wasn't getting on her nerves already. "Business is what I came here for, not pleasure."

Khabir nodded at her, then he waved her away after Deborah ordered a red wine. "So tell me, Showbiz, how does a man like you get passed up to receive his father's throne, and why was it given to your little brother?"

I felt anger surge through me right away. "Why you all in my bidness, kid?"

"Because I am looking to go into business with you. Before I am able to make that transition, I must find out what kind of man I am dealing with. Now answer the question."

"My father was an idiot. He favored my brother since birth, because of his undying love for her. It was never about me. When it came to the Vega throne, he felt that I wasn't ready for it because I was more wild and dangerous. My temper can be lethal, but whose isn't?" I mugged him.

"Before your father passed, he was indebted to Kosov and the Putins for a substantial amount of money. Tristian was able to straighten that debt in a short period of time. He was also able to meet your father's requirements for the Vega throne before you were able to. Why shouldn't he have been given it?"

"Because it was my muthafuckin' birthright. You see, I don't give a fuck about Chico Vega, nor Tristian. I am the king of the Vegas. That's how this shit go. Tristian stepped down, and I stepped up. That shit should've never gone to him anyway, but only children and bitches cry over spilled milk. As it stands today, I am Juanito Vega, King of the Vegas. Next phase." I slammed my hand on the table and made Deborah jump.

Khabir's guards pinned twenty different beams on me, before he waved his hand and they took their weapons off of me. "Talk to me about Bruno. What does he mean to you?"

"Nothing. Next question."

Khabir laughed. "I guess you are waiting for me to get to the nitty gritty, huh?"

"Yeah, that's what I am here for."

The maid came back and handed Deborah her drink. She sipped from it and looked over at Khabir. Khabir smiled and scooted to the edge of the couch. "Bruno is here in Dubai to also have a meeting with me. He is asking for protection from the Russians, and also for a five hundred million dollar bail out for the Gomez empire. It seems that Bruno had made one too many deals around the world, and now leaders are asking for either their money, or his demise. Me personally, I don't like the guy, nor his family."

"Oh yeah, and why is that?" I asked, eyeing him closely.

"Bruno and the Gomezes chose to stand behind Ahmad when he had the throne, prior to Khabir stepping on to it. Bruno also voted for the Chinese government to crush the Aziz family when they first jumped into the oil trade and made a few wrong turns. The Aziz family was close to bankruptcy until Khabir and I met in Saudi Arabia and I helped him to discover the work of Tech and investing. In a few short years, the Aziz family was able to accrue billions of dollars. He's been grateful ever since. The reason you sit here right now, Showbiz, is because he owes me a favor, and I feel it in my spirit to do right by the Vegas, even though technically it should be through Tristian. But as you've stated, he stepped down, and you stepped up. So here we are."

"Clear and cut enough for you?" Khabir smiled and stood up. "So, the Vegas fields are no more. Yet the Gomez fields are rich and plentiful. The only problem with that is that their fields are ruled by Vorsky and the Putins." He rubbed his chin. "You want to retire the Vegas. That only happens with money, and prestige. I need to crush Bruno for my own selfish reasons, but in order to make it worth your while, I must help you raise up your people and their standing in the world. I must also do this because us Azizes owe Deborah greatly. But the Russians are a tricky bunch of savages. So how will all of this unfold for the greater good of us all? Step one. Tomorrow night you are going to kill Bruno Gomez and bring me his head. After you complete this task, I will inform you of step two. We will accomplish all of these tasks that I will set forth before your vacation here in Dubai is over. In the meantime, enjoy yourself. And trust me, my word is everything." He stepped over and we shook hands again.

***

Deborah came onto the dock of the Yacht with her Victoria Secrets robe blowing in the wind. She held a bottle of Moët in her right hand, and a blunt in her left. It was a warm night, one where my head was all over the place. I was laid back on the bed after taking three Percocets. When she came into the room, I sat up shirtless.

"Hey baby." She leaned down and kissed me on the lips. "Why are you in here sulking? The Indians are about to let off a bunch of spectacular fireworks, and I want you to see this. It's one of the coolest things you've ever seen."

"I've seen fireworks before. Plus, I'm not in the mood for no celebratory shit. I need to get my head right so I can handle this business. I see the higher up you go in the game, the more this shit becomes confusing. I've been a dope boy and a murderer my whole life. This is a whole other facet of the game."

She sighed and sat beside me. "I know, baby. There are so many things that your father kept from you boys that I wish he wouldn't have, but I guess it was necessary. However, you are the king now, Showbiz. You are forced to do what it takes. The job of a king is like no other. All of the burdens of the Vegas will be on your shoulders. As much as I know you would like for things to be easier or clearer, they can't be. You are in a war to restore the Vegas. That's all you've ever wanted, and now you are getting your chance. You must seize this opportunity and capitalize off of it. I have you in the best position to succeed in this endeavor."

"That's another thing, mama, what is your agenda here? Why are you going so hard for me, all of the sudden? I thought you were pro Tristian?"

"I am, and I was." She shrugged her shoulders. "I guess I have a little confession to make. Do you remember back when your father made the stipulation of what it would take in order for one of his sons to take over the Vega throne, and you boys were forced to come up with fifteen million dollars in addition to acquiring the Red Hook Houses?

"Yeah, what about it?" I turned to look at her.

"Well, let's just say that I helped your brother. A lot, actually."

I stood up. "What?" Now I was heated. "You mean to tell me that you're the reason that he was able to make that deadline before me?"

102

"Baby, calm down. That's why I'm sitting here now, trying to right my wrongs for you. I know that you were rightfully deserving of the throne. But I made a mistake. He's my son, for God's sake."

Before I could even think about it, I was grabbing her by her neck and dragging her outside and onto the deck by it. I picked her up and hung her over the railing.

"This whole time you made me think that he was able to do some shit that I wasn't. You had my father thinking that Tristian was a better son than I was. Bitch, how could you?" I choked her with both of my hands with the intent to kill her, and there was nothing that was going to prevent me from doing so.

She slapped at my arms and hands, gagging as I choked her harder and harder. Her eyes rolled into the back of her head and I don't know why, but I let her go for a moment. I stood over her with my chest heaving up and down. She coughed and held her throat. I felt no mercy.

"You said I was yo' son. You were supposed to stay out of this." I picked her up, stormed back into the room with her, and threw her on the bed. "I'm 'bout to make yo' ass pay. You wanna fuck wit me? Cool."

Chapter 11

Deborah scooted back on the bed and held her hands up. "Baby, please calm down. Just wait for a second and hear me out." She sat on the edge of the bed and tucked her hair behind her ear. I could tell that she was ready to panic.

I took my Fendi button up off and slung it to the floor. Underneath it was an all-black beater. My shorts were expensive, so they were fitting me snug. I pulled the Gucci belt out of them, and wrapped the buckle around my hand. "Yo, you got a few seconds to convince me to not whoop yo ass. If you don't, I'm finna be the parent tonight, word to Jehovah."

She ran her fingers through her hair again. "Okay, baby, listen. To understand why I called myself intervening, you have to understand the kind of background that I come from."

"Bitch, yo time is running out. And I swear to God, I don't care about anything you about to tell me. This was the Vega's throne, and because of your meddling, you made my father pass me up for it. What the fuck yo background gotta do with that?"

She swallowed her spit again. "Baby, when I was little, all of my brothers, and my cousins were dope boys. They all were money hungry, hustling animals that chased millions of dollars at a time. Never thousands."

I whipped the belt through the air and slammed it on the bed right beside her. She jumped up. "Sit yo punk ass back down before I murder you in this mafucka. Sit down."

She did.

"Continue."

"All I've wanted ever since Tristian was born was for him to be king of somethin'. I wanted him to be the king of my side of his bloodline, but that wasn't the case. All of my brothers have married and went into other portions of the game.

Wall Street, real estate, Tech, foreign trade, things of that nature. And while doing so, they have one way or the other lost touch with the inner essence of our family. We are all doing our own thing. I wanted Tristian to be great. I wanted him to be better than every man in my family because it would've made it that much better, since I would've given birth to him. When your father, Chico, got sick, and he was looking for an heir, why would I have not thought to help my son gain his seat? It spelled power, money, and influence that spanned the globe. The Vegas, before their fall, were a name to revere. I wanted for Tristian to have that behind him. I knew that I could merge my connections with those of the Vegas, and together we could slowly take over the world."

"And what about me, bitch? Did you stop to think about the fact that your son was taking my birthright away from me? He made my father feel like I wasn't worthy to carry on a name and a throne that was rightfully mine. That's bogus. You got me fucked up. And since I care about you, I am not going to kill you. But tonight, I'm about to make yo' ass pay for your sins. Get the fuck up and lock that door. Right now."

Deborah fell to her knees and placed her hands together in prayer fashion. "Please, Juanito. You're my son. I love you. The reason we are here in Dubai is so I can right all of the ways that I hurt you or affected the Vega throne. Once you are acclimated alongside of Saudi Arabia, the sky will be the limit for the Vegas, and you will have been the one that came back to restore your people stronger than they have ever been before. You will be greater than Chico."

I nodded. "I hear all of that. Now get yo ass up and do like I say."

"But please." She got up on wobbly legs and walked to the door. When she got there, she stood looking out for a long

106

while. Then she slowly closed and locked the door. She turned around and faced me. She took a deep breath. "Now what?"

I dropped my shorts and pointed at the bed. "Get yo ass over here and lay across this bed."

She nodded and made her way over to me. She stood a short distance away from me. "You don't have to do this, Juanito."

"You didn't have to do what you did either. Do what the fuck I say."

She placed one knee on the bed. Her Versace dress raised on her thighs, and then the other one was up. "Whatever you are about to do to me, just don't kill me. I know that you are angry, but remember that I have always been like a mother to you." W Together for fifteen years, Jihad and Zena Thomas loved each other deeper than words could describe. They'd been through numerous obstacles together and in the end their love always prevailed. When trouble moves into their neighborhood their bond is put to the ultimate test. Their five year old son Jafarr is the glue that holds the family together but, when tragedy strikes the bond threatens to break. Zena loses all faith in Jihad, and it seems there is nothing he can do to restore that faith. Jihad makes a deal with a member of a deadly cartel to try to get his family ahead, when all goes wrong all the fingers point to him, now Zena is accusing her husband of murder, and her boss begins to take advantage of Zena's fragile mind set.

The head of the cartel lost his cool and killed a man in broad daylight, now a witness threatens his freedom by agreeing to testify for the federal government, now Armando Diaz puts all his energy into finding this witness, he won't hesitate to kill families to avoid prison. Now set on a collision course to cross paths with Jihad, a street gangsta turned family man. Both men are in a fight for their lives, and the lives of the ones they hold closest to their hearts. There are no rules as these two invisible enemies begin a war of revenge, in attempts to avenge lost loved ones. From the bullet riddled blocks of Chicago to the grimey streets of Gary, Indiana to gang infested small towns of Wisconsin the war between Jihad and Armando turns legendary with that said she laid down.

I placed the belt around my neck and walked over to her and yanked her dress up. Her light blue thong came on display. Her caramel colored ass cheeks were chubby, with light stretch marks going across them. Once her dress was up, I took the belt from around my neck. "Yo, when you fuck up like a kid, that's when you get yo ass whooped like one. I slashed the belt through the air and whacked her hard on her ass. She jumped up and rolled on to her side rubbing her ass.

"Oh my God. Oh my God. You actually hit me. You hit me. What's the matter with you, Juanito?"

Before she could even get any more words out of her mouth, I was whooping her ass like she was an unruly child, holding her arm while I did so. She tried to fight away from me. She tried to catch the belt, but that only made me hit her ass harder.

I thought about all of the hard work I had to put down in the slums, trying my best to come up with that fifteen million for my father's throne. All along, Tristian used Deborah to make me look like a got damn fool. I hated that nigga. He was a bitch. And because he was so soft and so weak, he was forced to run to a woman that was used to babying him, while a nigga like me was forced to get it out the mud. That was bullshit, and because of that, I was going to kill his ass. That was a guarantee. I blanked out, and when I came back to, I was tearing Deborah's ass up so bad that she was crying. She jumped up and ran into a corner holding her cheeks. My chest was heaving up and down like crazy. I was out of breath.

"You don't care about me, Juanito? There is no way that you care about me and you're able to beat me like you're doing," she cried with tears coming down her cheeks.

I dropped the belt and snatched her up, holding her against the wall. "Do you really know who I am?" I hissed.

"I thought I did, but I don't think I do. You're an animal. I can't believe you did me like this." She jerked away from me and wiggled out of my grasp. She pulled down her dress and picked up her purse. "I'm out of here. I'm still going to hold up my end of things for you with Khabir, but personally, I don't want anything else to do with you. We never have to speak again." She tried to walk past me.

I grabbed her and slammed her against the wall. My right hand was around her throat. My cheek rested up against hers. "Aw, so you think you running shit again, huh? What, you done got in your feelings? Do you know how many innocent people lost their lives because of the stunt you pulled?"

"I don't know, and frankly I don't give a fuck. Death is a part of the game. Every man that is a part of this world that we rotate in knows that. So spare me with the death and pity talk."

I tightened my grip a bit. "Aw, so now you tough? What, that li'l ass whoopin' toughened you up?"

"Do whatever you wanna do to me, Juanito. I'm done apologizing. I am sure that if Amelia was able to cut corners so she could put you in a position to win the throne, she would've done the same thing."

Amelia was my biological mother's name. She and Deborah had been rivals since high school because of their love for my father.

"Yeah, well she didn't cheat, but you did for Tristian, and because of that, you gotta answer for your sins." I slowly rubbed my hand down her dress until it was sunk into her crease. I could feel her heat.

T.J. Edwards

She closed her eyes. "I want to leave, Juanito. I need to be alone so I can collect my thoughts."

I pulled the dress over her hips and slipped my hand under it. I felt her panties, they were soaked. I forced the material into the lips and licked her neck slowly. "You were supposed to protect me, too, mama."

She shivered. "Shut up, Juanito, I'm ready to leave."

I sucked her neck and slid my right hand into her panties. My fingers separated her sex lips and sunk into her hole. She stood up on her tippy toes and moaned. "I still got mad love for you, mama, I'm still yo baby, and I still need you. Ain't nothing gon' change that." My fingers slipped in and out of her now. She rocked her hips forward and backward. Her juices dripped off of my digits.

"I don't wanna do this, Juanito. You shouldn't have whooped me like that. It hurt me." She shuddered when I picked her up and carried her to the bed. I tossed her on it and jumped on top of her. She held her arms straight out to stop me from sinking lower to create contact with my lips. "I am ready to go, Juanito. I ain't feeling this right now. Get the fuck off of me." She slapped me across the face.

I sat up, straddling her body. I was stunned. She tried to climb from under me, but I dropped my weight and held my face. My anger got the better of me. Suddenly, I snapped. I ripped her dress from her in one yank. It tore. I threw it over my shoulder. Next, I ripped her bra down the middle and tossed that as well. "See, I tried to be nice to yo ass, but you gon' bring this savage shit out of me." I forced myself between her thighs. Once there, I yanked her panties off in one tug, and lined myself up. She slapped me again. I wiggled from right to left and held her thighs in place. Then, with one curl of my back, I buried my dick deep into her pussy.

She gasped and arched her back. She scratched my chest. Then she fell back while I fucked her harder than I had ever fucked anybody in my life. I held her wrists pinned to the sides of her head and dug deeper and deeper into her, faster and faster, with no mercy.

"Baby. Baby. Unh. Unh. Shit. Awwww fuck." She put her ankles up and wrapped them around my waist while her big titties bounced up and down on her frame. She pulled her hard nipples.

"Huh. Huh. Huh. Huh. Fuck, this pussy so good. It's sooooooo good." I sped up and licked all over her nipples.

She laid back and allowed me to pound her out for fifteen minutes before she screamed and came all over me, shaking like crazy. "That's what this is all about. You just wanted to... Unnn. Unnn. Fuck me." She tried to sit up, but I was fuckin' her so hard and fast that it was impossible for her to do that. So she laid back down and pulled a pillowcase off of one of the pillows and started biting on it. She screamed into it and started to shake like crazy again.

I flipped her ass over onto her stomach and spaced her thighs. As soon as they were spaced, I fell between them, pushed her right knee to her ribs, and slipped back into her. I bit into her neck and dogged that ass, just like that. Her fat booty was like cushion every time it slammed into my lap." She began to claw at the bed.

"Baby. Baby. Son. Wait. Uhhhhhh fuck. You're killing me. You're killing me. Unnnn shit."

My tongue slipped into her mouth. I slurped and sucked on her lip while I fucked her harder and harder. She reached behind her and scratched my waist, and I came deep in her pussy, with spasms. I kept fucking for thirty more seconds, then plunged as deep as I could go and allowed my nut to leak into her. When I pulled him out, he was still rock hard. I climbed up to her and rubbed him on her lips. "Huh, ma."

She was breathing hard. Her eyes were slits. She opened her mouth and sucked me into her lips. Very slowly she sucked me, moaning and rubbing under her belly. She was laid on her side, sucking me like porn star. I slipped out of her lips and pulled her to all fours. I spread her ass and placed my face on her cheeks back there. My tongue licked circles around her rosebud. I dipped it into her and made sure that I slobbered all over it. When it was leaking along with her pussy, I got behind her and grabbed a handful of her hair. Her back dipped inward. I placed the head of my pipe right on her crinkle and forced him slowly into her.

"Unnnnn shit! You just flipping me." She laid her face on the bed and spaced her knees.

Slap.

"Unnn. Fuck, baby."

Slap.

"Yes. Shit yes."

I grabbed a hold of her hips and started to fuck her at full speed. That juicy booty bounced around like Jell-O every time I slammed into her. She moaned loud, and the louder she did, the faster I hit that ass, and the deeper I went, until she was gripping me with her anus, sending ripples through me.

"Fuck mama. Fuck me, baby. Fuck this ass. Uhhh. Baby. Unh. Unh." Her fingers pinched and rubbed her clit as fast as I was hitting her.

I stroked her for ten straight minutes, loving the fact that I was able to fuck my brother's mother's ass. I watched my dick go in and out of her, over and over, and then it became too much. I saw the way she was swallowing me, and I couldn't take it. I came. I pulled out and bussed all over her ass. Side walked on my knees and skeeted all over her face as well. She laid there shaking, out of breath, with her mouth wide open.

"Now we even." I slapped that ass and wiped my dick on her titties before jumping out of the bed and into the shower. My last sights were of her rubbing her pussy. Her nipples were rock hard.

***

When I made it back to the hotel that night, Mecca was waiting in the hallway for me. She had her arms crossed around her body, leaning up against the wall by the door. "Hey."

I stopped in front of her and looked her over. "What's the matter? Did you get a call from the homies out in New York? Are we under the gun? I had my phone off. I was handling some much needed business."

Deborah swiped her card into her door behind me. "Good night, baby. Good night to you, too, Mecca." She smiled, stepped into her room, and closed the door.

Mecca sighed. "You were with her tonight, weren't you?"

I avoided her eyes. "Yo, did somethin' happen back in the Apple or what?"

"You can't even look at me. Wow. Nall, it's all good. Although, Kammron did make another move. Supposedly, he's linking up with some killas out of Yonkers or something. They just up a few decks over on Bradbury Ave and 139th. But don't worry, I already sent killas over there to break that shit up. I should be getting a report back any hour now." She walked away from me and mugged Deborah's door. "Yo, what's good wit' you and this old broad. I know she ain't really acting like your mother when I ain't around. But what, are y'all in a relationship or somethin'?"

"Mecca, it's late and you're bugging right now. You need to get some sleep. Come over here and give me a hug."

"Nall, I ain't on that right now. I just wanted to make sure that you were okay, since you weren't answering your phone. Since I see that you are, I'm about to turn in and call it a night. You have a good one."

"Mecca, bring yo ass over here and give me my mafuckin' hug. Now." I stepped closer to her.

She remained in her tracks with her head down. Slowly but surely she began to make her way over to me, but then my suite's door opened and Kalani stepped into the hallway. "Showbiz Vega, why you ain't been answering your phone? Do you have any idea how worried I was about you?"

"Yeah, Showbiz, do you?" Mecca faced me away from Kalani and rolled her eyes. "Good night." She slid her key card into her door, stepped inside, and closed it back.

Kalani grabbed a hold of my wrist and pulled me into the room. "While you were out doing your thing, I ordered this lingerie, and you gotta see me in it. I got somethin' for your ass tonight. I promise you. Watch this."

I was stuck. For the first time in my life, I was sick over wondering how I'd made another person feel. I wanted to talk to Mecca. I needed to make sure that she was straight. But after using the bathroom and excusing myself from Kalani to go and get ice, I knocked on Mecca's door, and she ignored me. No matter what I said, or what I did, that night, she left me out in the hallway. I left from in front of her door both angry and confused. Angry because I felt disrespected and confused because I couldn't get her ass out of my mind, even while Kalani modeled one of the sexiest pieces of lingerie that I had ever seen. I couldn't enjoy it, and we argued the rest of the night because I was unable to fuck her. But I didn't care. Mecca had me mentally somewhere else.

Chapter 12

"To what do I owe this pleasure?" Bruno Gomez asked as soon as he stepped into the den of Khabir's palace with his son, Chulo Gomez, walking behind him. Bruno was five feet six inches tall, golden colored, with a big bald spot in the middle of his head, and wavy hair around the sides. Chulo was a spitting image of his father, yet he had long wavy hair, and he hadn't started to go bald just yet.

Khabir stood up wearing a Dolce and Gabbana silk shirt and cotton shorts that were snugger than they should have been. He extended his hand, and they shook up. He directed Bruno to have a seat at the long table. His and Chulo's chairs were already pulled out. They sat directly across from me and Mecca. Chulo shook Khabir's hand and then sat beside his father. Khabir then took his seat.

"So, you've made your way to the bosses table. What, are you here to ask for a hand out to uplift the Vegas?" Bruno laughed. "It's going to take a lot more than a hand." He looked up at Khabir. "Why is he here? And who is she?" He looked at Mecca.

Khabir waited until a thick ass Arab sista, with long black hair, dressed in a sarong that clung to her dark golden colored body, finished pouring orange juice into his chalice. He held his silence. She then walked out of the room with her ass shaking and closed the door. That bitch was bad. Khabir sipped his drink and sat back in his chair.

"Bruno, whenever you come to my palace, the first thing you must know is that you aren't running the show, I am. You must secondly greet each one of my guests with respect. Thirdly, you never question me, or my reasoning behind anything that I do here. And finally, you are to never insult, or disrespect, those that are sitting around this table. As it stands, you have managed to break each one of these rules, so I think that an apology is in order. First to myself, and then to Mr. Vega and his accomplice. I believe her name is Mecca."

Chulo frowned his face. "You, you can't talk to my pops like that. I don't know who you think you are, but he is Bruno Gomez, the great."

"No, it's okay, son. What's right is right," Bruno began.

"But, Papi, the way he spoke to you is..."

"Chulo, silence. I got this." Bruno snapped, holding up his hand. He looked up to Khabir. "Mr. Aziz, I apologize for my disrespect." He looked over to me and lowered his eyes. "I don't know how you are able to sit at this table right now, but you're here. Khabir, I apologize for offending this guest right here, and her. There, you happy?"

Khabir sipped out of his orange juice. "Now that we are all here, I think it is time that we talk business."

"What business could he possibly have to talk with you? The Vegas are broke. They don't have any more fields that the Russians don't own. And as far as I know, he isn't the king of the Vegas. So unless he is acting as an ambassador for their bloodline, he is here on fraudulent terms."

I laughed at that. "You see, Bruno, that's where you are wrong. I am the king of the Vegas, and we have over four hundred acres of cocaine, and two hundred of heroin."

"That's a got damn lie. I've rolled through your fields lately. They are demolished. You have no more than twenty acres left, and they no longer belong to you, they are considered Russian property. You are a fraud. Besides isn't Tristian Vega the rightful replacement to Chico Vega?"

Now I was getting downright heated. He saw this and smiled. I sat back in my chair and tried to remain as calm as I could, just waiting on my moment.

"Khabir, as you know, our families haven't gotten along since the beginning of time. I was summoned here to talk business with you, but there is no way that I can carry on with this fraud in the room. I will be in Dubai three months from tomorrow, we will talk then." He stood up.

Khabir slammed his hand on the table so loud that I jumped back. "Sit your ass down, Bruno. Sit the fuck down, right now, and don't get your broke ass back up until I give you the order to. Now sit."

Bruno hesitated. He turned beet red. He looked down at a heartbroken Chulo. "Broke? Dad, what is he talking about?"

I smiled. "Yo pops done got in way over his head. He's a horrible investor. And he owes so many countries money that the reason he brought his broke ass here is because he is looking for a bail out. Yeah." I wiped my mouth with my fingers. "This goofy ass nigga is looking for a bail out from the same mafucka that he didn't want on the Aziz throne to begin with."

"Dad, is this true? Is what this scorned Vega saying the truth?" Chulo asked.

"You've discussed my affairs with him. How does he know these things, Khabir?" Bruno started to shake.

Khabir pointed to his chair. Bruno sat, and kept his eyes pinned on Khabir. Khabir stood up. "It's public record. Your affairs, I mean. All of those that are in the Narcotics business globally know about your destitute state. Your fields, and your family, are a constant conversation. Mr. Vega doesn't have any information that any connected player in this game doesn't already have." Khabir sipped from his orange juice again. "You're in a fucked up position, Bruno. What are you going to do?"

Just then, the doors to his boardroom opened. Deborah held them open while two short Chinese men entered the room. They stopped in front of Khabir and bowed to him before they shook hands. The men were wearing blue doctor's masks over their faces. They took a seat to the left of Khabir.

Bruno jumped up. "Mr. Woo, Mr. Jung, I-I-I was on my way to China after I left this business meeting of sorts."

Mr. Woo held up his hand. "You were given a time length by our regime. You failed. There is no more need for words. We are here for the show, and to appease Mr. Aziz."

Mr. Jung pointed at Bruno. "You are FILTH. Nothing more." He balled his hand into a fist and banged it on the table.

Deborah sat beside me. She was also wearing a doctor's mask. The same Arab sista from before came into the room and placed a golden colored tool box on the table. She bowed to the Chinese and backed out of the room. My eyes were pinned on her fat ass again. It looked so good.

Bruno sat down. "What is the meaning of all of this? Why am I really here? What show are they talking about?"

Khabir was very calm. "When it comes to the narcotics world, it goes one hand washes the other. There is no way for any major player to be able to thrive in it unless he is able to share goods and services with all of the other players in the game. If you are unable to be used in this world, then you are useless. It is about more than money when you reach this height. It is about respect, honor, loyalty, and the powers that reach across the aisle to you, and vice versa.

"In this case, the Aziz family has entered into a sacred contract with the Chinese government. One of the stipulations of our contract is to remedy the situation that the Gomezes have done in financially wronging their Empire. In exchange for our remedying that situation, they will whisper in the ears of the Putin regime and get them to leave the islands and their hold on the narcotics trade down that way. This will free up a limitless income for both the Chinese empire, and the Aziz."

"That's great, Khabir. With Vorsky out of the way I will be able to go into overdrive for you and the Chinese. You guys will have your money back in two years' time with a fifty percent interest."

Khabir opened the tool box and slid it in front of me. "Now, you see, that's where things get tricky. In order for this contract to work on all sides, the Gomez family, as we know them, must be crushed. And what better way to have them as such than to allow their longtime rivals to do it? An ousted son of the Vegas, just like I was an ousted son by the Aziz, before Ahmad was crushed. You supported him. You funded his regime, and because of your dollars, my mother, my sister, and all eight of my brothers were killed. But here I stand as king of the throne. My father chose Ahmad, but I chose me."

As soon as he said that, I hopped on the table, grabbing a steel blade deer hunting knife out of the tool box. I'd had my eye on it the entire time. My Jordans squeaked against the surface of the varnished wood. I jumped into Bruno's lap and slashed him across the face ten quick times before we fell to the floor with him hollering and screaming. Bloodshot all across my neck and cheek. I slashed him ten more times and jumped up. Chulo got ready to attack me but Mecca saw it and jumped over the table, slamming a scalpel into his neck. He hollered and stumbled backward. He pulled it out and the hole began to shoot out blood, over and over, as if it were a broken pipe.

"Chop his head off in front of the Chinese. They have come a long way for this show, Juanito." Khabir ordered with his eyes big.

I grabbed a hold of Bruno's sparse hair and slammed him face first on the table. I took a mini saw out of the tool box while Bruno struggled against me with a losing effort. I pinned him just right. To my left, Mecca sat on Chulo's chest stabbing

119

him, over and over, in the face. She raised the scalpel all the way over her head and brought it down hard into his right eye, and then stood up, breathing hard. She saw us and helped me to pin Bruno down so that his face was sideways on the table, but his neck was hanging just off of it. Her face was covered in Chulo's blood. I took the saw and began to cut slowly.

"Awwwww. Awwwww. Help me. Help me. Awwwww. You mother fucker," he screamed, and kicked his legs wildly.

"Shut up." Mecca kneed him in the balls and held him tighter.

The Chinese clapped their hands and drank liquor from their shot glasses. I cut into Bruno's neck until the blade sunk deep inside of it. From there, I picked up the speed. Blood popped into the air and got all over the table. I cut harder, feeling the saw grind against his gristle and bone before it cut through to the other side. The weight of my body caused me to fall forward. Bruno's body dropped to the floor, and his head rolled along the table. I caught my balance and took a hold of it in my hands. I bowed before the Chinese.

Khabir came and stood beside me. He placed his hand on my back and nodded to me. He snapped his fingers, and the same Arab sista from before took the head out of my hands and dropped it into a special Ziploc bag. Another female, equally sexually, came into the room, and opened a big cooler. The first Arab sista placed the head into the cooler and slid it across the table to the Chinese.

They stood up, bowed at us, grabbed the cooler, and left the room, followed by the two Arab women. Khabir smiled and stepped into my face.

"The burden of annihilating the Gomez family is on you now. The Russians will never mess with you again. Forty percent of everything you make in those fields belong to the Aziz. I will straighten the Chinese, and the Russians. But you, King

Juanito Vega, will report to me. Do we understand each other?"

"Yeah, I do."

"Awright, let's get this place cleaned up." Khabir patted my back and walked toward the door.

"Wait a minute. Was all that stuff that you said about being passed up for your father's throne, and ousted by the Aziz, before you came back to crush your brother for your rightful place true?"

"Every word of it." He laughed. "As soon as Deborah here told me your story, I was all in. You and I have a lot in common, but our communication will be short until you can prove to me what this blessing means to you. You now officially have enough might to restore your people. The next move you make should be to take a hold of the Gomez fields and rename them. Secondly, you have to play the political game. Judges, Senators, hell, even the Vice President, if not the president himself. You have to become a part of these people. You must invade their spaces. The political game is how families become dynasties. That is the last bit of wisdom I will impart on you. Peace, my brother, and long live King Juanito Vega."

***

That night I sent a hundred members of the Vega Bloods through Havana, Cuba to crush the rest of the surviving Gomez family. The Russians stood down and allowed the atrocities to occur. Sixteen hours later, I got word that the massacre had been a success. I laid in bed with a wide smile on my face. It was all coming into existence.

Chapter 13

The day we got back to New York just so happened to be Mecca's eighteenth birthday. It was July the twenty ninth, hot and humid. It was so hot that I felt like I couldn't breathe when I stepped off of the plane. We jumped into an air conditioned limousine that escorted both Kalani and Deborah to the Trump towers, where they went inside and stayed in the rooms that were reserved for us. I took the limo with Mecca still inside of it and went to get her the birthday present that I felt a queen like her should get from a boss ass nigga like me.

Her eyes lit up when I walked her across the car lot and stopped her in front of her present. "No. No, Showbiz. Are you kidding me?" She exclaimed with her hands to the side of her cheeks.

"Yes, yes, yes. This is a twenty-twenty Bugatti Chiron. This mafucka ran me two point nine million dollars, and because you fuckin' wit' me the long way, and helped me to step up on this throne, this bitch is yours. Congratulations, you now rolling harder than any other bitch in New York. Nall, fuck that, America, period." I had to flex one time. The sun reflected off of my Chanel glasses, and the gold around my neck.

The diamonds in Mecca's ears sparkled in the light. She made a revolution around the black and white car and opened the door, taking a seat inside. The interior was all pink soft leather. It looked like a command center for NASA on the inside. She ran her hand over the dashboard, and then the steering wheel. She got behind it and started the ignition. It hummed and came to life. I was cheesing like a mafucka. She looked up to me with her eyes watery. "This is too much. I can't accept it."

I squatted down, even though I didn't like the thought of wrinkling my Jordans. I took a hold of her chin. "Yo, you're a Vega Queen now. The muthafuckin' world is mine, and therefore, it is yours. We in this shit together. I know you been struggling your whole life, but fuck that now. You my baby, and I love yo li'l ass. You hear me?"

She nodded. "Yes. But where will I park it? The people in the projects will steal it ASAP."

"Yo, didn't you just hear me say that I run the world now? Huh? You ain't about to stay in no projects no more. Your new residence will be in the Hamptons, with me. You about to have your own shit. That bitch, Deborah, is a real estate mogul. She already got you in escrow."

She blinked tears. "So what do I do? What about my mother?"

"We gon' get her right, too. But for right now, fuck everybody. Today is your day. Let's make this shit about you." As we were talking, a salesgirl drove a black on black twenty-twenty Chiron Sport up beside me and got out.

"You're all set, Mr. Vega. I hope you enjoy your vehicles." The blond haired, blue eyed woman said before clicking her high heels on the pavement, walking away from us, with her flat booty. I turned my nose up. The sexiest part of her was the red bottoms she was rocking. "Yo, gon' and pull off, I'ma follow you."

***

Mecca put the pedal to the metal as she flew down the highway in her drop top, with her arm resting on the window seal. Her long pretty hair blew in the wind. I nodded my head to the Dave East track bumping out of my speakers. My top was dropped like a bitches at Mardi Gras, and I was feeling better than a nigga that had just gotten some pussy for the first time. The wind felt good on my face, and the Bugatti I was rolling cost me three million and some change. But I didn't give no fuck because I was Showbiz Vega. The Gomez fields belonged to me and my new age Vega Bloods. I was king of the world and wasn't nobody about to shit on my parade without suffering the ultimate consequences.

***

When I made it to the hotel to pick Kalani up, she flipped out. She jogged into the parking lot and stopped in front of Mecca's whip. "What the fuck is this? Whose shit is this?" Her eyes were bucked. She mugged me.

Mecca stayed in the car.

Kalani walked over to me and looked over my Bugatti. "Daddy, that little girl is driving a Chiron. That car is almost three million dollars. They've only made a few of them for the upper crust of the world. How in the hell is she driving one that is the bitch to yours? Is it mine and she just drove it here for me?"

I sat on the hood of my shit and went through my text messages on my iPhone. "It's her birthday. She just turned eighteen. That bitch hitting, ain't it?"

"Juanito Showbiz Vega, I don't give a fuck if she just turned eighty. You got this yellow ass bitch rolling around New York City in a whip that even Cardi B ain't got yet. I'm supposed to be yo mafuckin' baby girl. If anybody rolling a whip that matches yo' fly, it's supposed to be me. Get yo pretty ass back in yo whip and go get my shit. I ain't playin'."

"They only had two of these bitches in the United States right now. I bumped out two music moguls to get these. If you ever get one of em', it ain't gon' be today." I put my phone back up.

"You think this shit is a game, don't you? Boy, don't you know that I am the worst kind of jealous female. Me seeing this girl in some shit that I want is making me think of doing some devious things to y'all. Yo, Juanito, fix this, Dunn, word up. I'm starting to feel like you're trying to squeeze me out. Hell hath no fury, nigga, word up, that's all I'm saying." She held up her middle finger to Mecca and got into my Bugatti with her Birkin bag in her lap.

***

That night, me and Mecca wanted to celebrate her birthday, so I shut down the Forty Forty club and invited all of the Vega Bloods. We closed the doors, once all of my killas were there, and I had the bottle girls bring out ten cases of Moët and ten cases of Ace of Spades. I hired strippers that were born and bred in Harlem and made sure that all of the Vegas didn't have nothing less than five.

One wall was lined up with top notch cuisines, while on the other side, it was all soul food. I'm talking collard greens, corn bread, fried chicken and fish, baked macaroni, you name it, I supplied it. We had the stage set up, and the locals from Harlem rocked the mic, both with rap and R&B. The dance floor was packed, and there was so much security outside that from the outside looking in, you would have sworn that the president himself was inside.

Kalani neglected to come, and that was cool with me. I placed my arm around Mecca and kept kissing her cheek all night. She kept her arm around my waist and laid her head on my shoulder. Her hair, nails, and diamonds were fresh. She wore a Tiara bussed down in pink and yellow diamonds that read Queen across the front of it.

She took a sip from her bottle of Moët and looked up at me with a smile on her gorgeous face. "Yo, Biz, word to Harlem, this is the nicest thing that anybody has ever done for me, ever since I've been alive. I got mad love and honor for you, kid."

I laughed. "You're my li'l baby. You already know I got you for the rest of our lives. Seeing as you're younger than me, that means until I kick the bucket."

"Seven years, wow. Big freaking deal." She rolled her eyes. "I love you, though."

"I love you, too. And this the first time that I've ever said it to anybody and actually meant it. You my mafuckin' heart. I ain't gon' play about you. You are officially the Queen of the Vegas. You should feel honored."

"I do, thank you, Showbiz. Damn, you drive me crazy." She hugged me tightly and looked up at me again. "Let's dance. I gotta show you this new Harlem shit, and I ain't talking about the shake either." She Milly rocked on to the dancefloor and I followed her, laughing.

I was high as a bitch off of Mollie, Percocets, and Robitussin, but no heroin. I was determined to kick that habit, and so far so good. After acting a fool for a full thirty minutes, the DJ switched the track to some slow music. I held Mecca close and rested my cheek against hers. "Yo, on my mother, I think that you are the finest woman in this room right here. When you are in my presence, all I wanna do is make you happy. That shit sounds too soft coming from a king?"

She shook her head. "Nope. I love when you talk to me like I know you ain't never talked to nobody else before. I need to hear it because sometimes I get so down on myself. I mean, I know what my role is, but you be having me feeling a way about you. Sometimes it's hard for me to keep my emotions out of this relationship, and I already know that it is business over feelings."

"You muthafuckin' right, li'l baby, but not when it comes to me and you. It's okay for us to love each other, and blend the two, as long as we know when and where it's appropriate. I'm crazy about you, and I'm the king. I know how to balance both, and I know when I am focusing too much time on one or the other."

"You see, that's where my problem lies. I find it hard to balance both. I mean, I know I'll get better, but for now you got me feeling like a princess. And I ain't never had that before because my daddy was never there. My mother treated me like shit because of what he did to her. And the only thing I remember about him is that my mother gave me this long scar because she said that I looked too much like him, and when she saw me, she saw him. So she took a box cutter and did this when I was eight years old."

I paused for a second and eyed the scar. I ran my finger over it, before kissing it with my lips. "Yo, fuck them, li'l baby. I got you now. You belong to me, and I ain't gon' fail you. I'd kill a nigga ass dead over you, Mecca, word to heaven."

"I know you would, and that's why I love you so much." She laid on my chest with a smile across her face.

***

After the dance, the show crew sang Happy Birthday to her, and gave her a bunch of gifts. Most consisted of guns, weed, jewelry, and knots of cash. After that was over, we ate. Then she got a few lap dances from the strippers, both the male and female ones, before we danced again. We wound up later that night in a helicopter, flying over Harlem with my arm around her.

"You see all of that shit down there, Goddess? That's ours. Mines and yours. We about to set the city on fire." We made two revolutions around Uptown and discussed going to the island of Cuba in the near future. I explained our history and told her about a lot of the things that we had been through. I explained what was going on with the newly conquered Gomez fields. I spoke to her about what was to come, and how the future was going to be a lot brighter than our past.

After the helicopter ride, we wound up on the top floor of the Trump Towers, making love in the bed on the balcony, under the stars, while the wind whistled loudly around us. We got down for three straight hours, until we were exhausted. We collapsed in the bed and didn't wake up until the next morning, when the sun came up. It was at that time that I knew for sure that Mecca had my cold heart, and I didn't know how to feel about that.

Chapter 14

With the advice from Khabir bouncing through my head like a bowling ball, I went on the prowl to solidify political connections. Judges were easy. For fifty thousand dollars a year, I would be able to have any federal judge that operated out of the New York sector in my back pocket is what Deborah told me. I bought three of them, two federal and one state. With all of the shit that me and the Vegas were doing, if we were brought down, I couldn't ever see us going in front of a state judge. All of the illegal activities that we took part in were federal, but I copped a state judge just in case. When it came to the game, it was always better to be safe than sorry.

After Deborah paid their wages up front, I met with a liaison for each official. I was told that for the duration of the time I had ties to these officials, we would always communicate through the liaison. I was cool with that, as long as they held up their end of the bargain. I was sure that they would after Deborah acquired their home addresses, and even the addresses of their summer and winter houses. I was given information on all of their vacation hot spots, and more than once, I made my presence known by visiting their communities just to drive by with a nice nod of the head to them. No words were ever exchanged, but there was no need for them anyway. I was sure that they got my gist.

Deborah said that a Senator was a little harder to acquire because they often dealt with major companies that were lining their pockets with millions of dollars at a time. I was just starting to build the Vegas from the ground back up, millions of dollars weren't really at my disposal, so I would have to step my game up before I was able to make that real transition into the government. While it was hard to find a senator that was willing to cross over for any less than five million dollars, or six months' worth of protection at a time, Deborah had a connection into the Cuomo family that I found useful, and highly beneficial.

Cuomo was the new Governor of the state of New York, and he was a grumpy, red-faced Italian, who was pig-headed and made sure that everything was run exactly the way that he wanted it to be run. His family circle consisted of a loving wife and four daughters that were his pride and joy.

On paper, Cuomo seemed like the perfect citizen. Before becoming governor he was active in the community of Staten Island, raised millions of dollars for an array of cancer organizations, and helped to bridge the educational gap when it came to the inner city youths of New York, and those that were suburban and privileged. He was elected in a landslide, and all of this closest circle was sure that his next step was going to be president of the United States of America. Cuomo seemed to be the perfect man without a chink in his armor. That was until Deborah found one.

***

A month after we'd all gotten back from Dubai, Deborah picked me up in a white Wraith early one Sunday morning, and rolled with me over to New Jersey with a sly smile on her face. She had her curly hair pulled back into a ponytail, and her red Chanel dress made her look gorgeous. Her makeup was done just right, and she smelled amazing. She looked over at me and batted her eyelashes. "Don't you look handsome this morning?"

Not only did I feel grumpy because I felt like I'd been awakened out of my sleep, but I had no idea what she wanted so early in the morning. Since she was always plugging me with something, I knew it was in my best interest to just roll with the punches. "Yo, it's six in the morning. I got a pounding ass headache, and I feel like I need another four hours of sleep before I fly back down to Havana. What's good?"

She shrugged her shoulders. "Why does something have to be good? Maybe I wanted to see you. Would that be so wrong?"

I laid back and looked out of the window. "Yo, if you looking for me to wax that ass right now, the kid is depleted. You gon' have to let me take a short nap, then I'll be able to get all up in that vet pussy that's been driving me crazy ever since my childhood." Now my stomach was hurting a little bit. I had to piss. How the fuck did I forget to piss before I left?

She looked over at me and stuck her bottom lip out like a little girl. "Juanito, I'm starting to feel unwanted by you. And after all of the things that I do for you. I shouldn't be feeling like this." She took my hand and placed it on her stomach. "There are two parts to the reason I got you up so early, the first thing is going to blow your mind. First, know that I do not need you involved, and I don't need any help. I am closing in on eighty million dollars, and my cosmetics company's stock is up by sixty percent. Also, the only reason I am telling you this is because it is your right to know, that's it. Do you understand that?"

I took my hand away and nodded. "Yeah, mama, I got you. But like I said, what's good?"

She was quiet and kept rolling down the highway for a moment. Then, after paying the toll, she turned to me. "Baby, I am pregnant, and it's your child. I am thankful for this baby because they told me that because of my age it would be harder for me to get pregnant, but I am, and I am so happy. No matter what you say, I am having this baby, and that's that. Any words?"

I was too busy mugging her ass. "Shorty, you old as a ma-fucka. How are you pregnant?"

"First of all, I'm forty five. That's not old. Watch yo' mouth. Secondly, boy you been dumping so much seed up in me every time that we are alone together. What did you think was going to happen?"

"I thought that you were too old to get pregnant. Yo, I ain't fuckin' around wit' no kid right now. I gotta get my shit together first, then I can focus on a child, and not until then."

"Li'l boy, you ain't talkin' to no little ass girl. I'm old, remember. I don't need you to be there for my child. I am rich, and beyond independent. I just wanted to let you know. You're still free. When you see this belly beginning to stick out, you'll know why." She rubbed it. "I'm so happy."

I let my window down and didn't care about her air conditioner. I needed some fresh air. I hung my arm out of the window and tried to calm down. "Yo, that's good that you're happy, Deborah. I'm willing to do whatever you need me to. Excuse my talk from earlier."

"Biz, I ain't studding you. I'm happy. I got everything in this world that I've ever wanted. I feel all that was missing was a newborn. I wanted another one with your father, but then Miguel happened with Amelia. Things ain't been right ever since. But you, Juanito. You're so healthy, and so fine. You are two times as gorgeous as the great, Chico Vega. I know that this baby will be the envy of everybody, and I'm going to love it to death." She kept rolling.

"What about Tristian?"

"What about him?"

"Will you tell him about the child?"

"Of course, it is going to be his sibling."

"So what do you think he is going to say when he finds out that his brother has his mother pregnant?"

"I didn't say I was going to tell him who the baby was with. That would be ignorant of me to do such a thing. For now, it'll be our little secret. How does that sound?"

"Yo, it is what it is. I know I'm finna be beating that pregnant pussy up. You already got a shot on you. With that kid inside of you, I can only imagine how good that shit is going to be."

She shook her head. "Tsk. Tsk, Juanito. All you care about is pussy. Damn, the consequences of slanging that trunk of yours all over town. One day that tool between your legs is going to be your downfall."

"Until then, I'm be hitting this pussy right here." I slipped my hand between her thighs and pat her juicy pussy through her panties. The heat radiated right onto my fingers.

"Are you ready for me to tell you the second reason why I brought you out this morning?"

I slipped my finger through the leg hole and into her hole. She opened her knees wider and moaned. I stroked the finger in and out of her. "Yeah, gon' head."

"Right now as we speak, I am sewing up a political force. This person has enormous power and reach. Where he is now, isn't where he is going to wind up two years from now, trust me." She moaned and arched her back. Her tongue traced her lips.

I pulled my finger out and sucked it into my lips. "Oh yeah, and why is this person willing to do business with me?"

She pulled her panties back over her sex lips. "Damn, you got me leaking. Hand me a wet wipe out of the glove box."

"Siri, open the glovebox," I ordered. Siri repeated the command and opened the box. It slowly came down. I grabbed a wet wipe and gave it to her.

"I recently linked arms with house representative Ocastio. She is on the front lines fighting the sex trafficking epidemic that is taking place in Central America. In two months, we have been able to bust more than a hundred men in the act and returned a thousand little girls back to their homes or helped them to gain citizenship here in America."

"And?"

"And that is enough said. Just know that I love you, and this is your final gift from me. I am moving to Paris at the end of the month. I want to be free and far away from the Apple. It is time that I live good and my spirit soars with the freedoms it craves."

"What, what does that mean?"

She laughed. "One day you will understand. For now, just be thankful."

***

When we bust through the door with Deborah's eight camera men, along with her, me, and Ocastio. Cuomo nearly jumped out of his skin. He was being rode by one naked girl that was so young that she didn't have any breast. She looked frail. There was another girl that he had his hand between her thighs, and another lying beside him that he was kissing. Two more were also in the bed naked with him, sitting along the headboard, with their thighs wide open, exposing themselves. Deborah's crew began to take picture after picture. The room flashed over and over again.

Cuomo jumped up out of the bed naked. "Hey, what's the meaning of this? What's going on?" He hollered.

Deborah waved for the cameras to stop flashing. They left the room, along with Ocastio. Only she and I remained. The little girls remained uncovered and seemed unaffected by our intrusion. Deborah stuck her finger in his face. "I told you to never deny me. Now look, I have you by the balls."

His eyes were wild. "What do you want? How did you get in here, for Christ's sake?"

"This is Juanito Vega, King of the Vegas. You are familiar with the family, no?"

He eyed me, worried like. "I am."

"From this point forward, you and he are locked in. Get acquainted with this young man because he is destined to be a force within the world. You play ball, or your career is over. You got me?"

He nodded. "Y-y-yeah, but the pictures? The girls? What about all of them?"

"Nothing more than insurance. Enjoy your evening."

And we left, just like that. I found out that Deborah had plugs into Cuomo's security. She had dirt on every one of them, and they broke their necks to do favors for her. After that day, Cuomo and I became comrades. I never respected him because I knew what he liked to do in his downtime, but to have a governor on your team was like having the Holy Grail to a billion dollars. I jumped into the game harder than ever, and New York was on notice.

T.J. Edwards

Chapter 15

"Yo, Showbiz, I've been thinking. I need to keep shit real wit' you, and let you know that I ain't ready to step down from the Vega throne," Tristian said, walking up behind me one rainy day in August. It was our father, Chico's, birthday. He had a black Fendi hoodie pulled over his head, and he smelled like Brut Cologne, which had been my old man's favorite fragrance.

There were twenty of the Vega Blood niggas lined up to the right of my father's tombstone. All wore all black and water resistant gray Timbs. I had on the same attire, as well, as a show of solidarity. When Tristian walked up, I had my head bowed, paying my respects. But after hearing that, I couldn't help but to turn around and look him dead on. "Fuck you say, Tristian?" Rain popped off of my hood, and the lightning lit up the sky. Loud thunder growled in the dark sky. The wind caused the rain to spray my face like a violent water hose.

"Yo, I ain't come here to get all of this shit with you. I just been thinking, that's all." He had ten Brooklyn niggas behind him. Every time I looked over his shoulder, they couldn't even look me in the eye. I knew killas when I saw them, and I wasn't getting that vibe from more than half of his crew.

"Aw, now you wanna jump back over and try to man the ship, now that I've done put all of this work in. I took over the Gomez fields from the Russians, and I got them bitches popping like never before. I got gardeners back on the Vega fields replanting and harvesting already. The Vega mansion, where our grandparents first came home to after their wedding day, is being re-built from the ground up. I have established a partnership with the Castros that are in power, something that not even Chico Vega was able to do. I am contributing to the economy of Cuba and helping with progressive trade. We are building schools for the underprivileged and helping to make sure that the entire island is able to have clean drinking water. Once again, the Vega name is starting to be revered and respected. Yet you think that this is the right time to try and claim my birthright? A birthright that you stole with the help of your mother?"

Tristian took a step back. He looked shocked that I would know so much. "Look, Showbiz, before Pop died, he left me in charge. He blessed me as the head. That means that I am the king of the Vegas, and there is nobody that can take that away from me. I appreciate what you have done for our family this far, but I'm sorry to say that the most I can offer you is a seat at my right hand." He turned to walk away from me.

I slapped my hand on his shoulder. "Tristian, wait. Are you serious? You would allow me to sit on your right, while you rule our people?"

"Of course, Showbiz. You are my brother, and the only one that I have left. What you have done for the Vegas this far has been legendary. I need your guidance and assistance in certain areas. I would love to have you upon this throne with me."

I looked into his eyes and placed my hand on his shoulder. "This is somethin' that we need to talk further about. I have a lot of investors within our family now that you will need to be introduced to. The game is no longer about cash in hand. It's stocks, bonds, foreign trade, and real estate, here and abroad. The Vegas work through political and foreign connections. The American dollar is becoming weak. I have been investing in the Yen and the Euro. These investments are the things that will insure that the Vegas have generational wealth and prestige."

"And these are the things that I will need for you to teach me about, beside me, as my right hand."

King of New York 5

Every time he said something about his right hand, I felt like I was seconds away from blowing his bitch ass head off. What the fuck was his problem? How dare he come and say something like this to me? I was Juanito Showbiz Vega, the greatest Vega to ever do it. "Little brother, what about your family? I heard that your son just had his second birthday. How is he?"

"He is well, so is Perjah. They are healthy and strong, more than I could ever ask for. Thank you for asking. And Kalani? How is she?" He curled his lip.

I laughed. "She just pussy, nigga. Why would you ask me about her?"

He shrugged his shoulders. "I don't know. Just seem to me like you got a thing for fuckin' wit the women that your family done already had. Including my mother." He scoffed. "You had the nerve to get her pregnant. What the fuck is wrong with you?"

Mecca locked eyes with me and winced. She looked off, and I mugged Tristian. "What the fuck is you talking about? Your mother ain't pregnant, and if she is, it ain't by me. We might've fooled around a little bit, but it ain't never got that serious as to where I was able to cum in her." I lied, knowing I'd bussed in Deborah over fifty times. She had that snapper. What could I say?

"Yeah, well it's still gross. I never lusted after Amelia. That was my father's baby's mother, and my brother's mama? What type of man would that make me?"

I shrugged my shoulders. "I don't know, and I don't give a fuck. What's done is done. I fucked both of those broads that you are jaded about, but ain't nan one of them got my seed. Yo mother lying."

He nodded. "Yeah, I bet. It is what it is, though. As long as I got Perjah, I'm good. She is the only queen that's worthy

141

to sit on the Vega throne beside me. You lucky I don't take shit personal when it comes to this empire shit. If I did, I wouldn't even be offering you a right hand slot. I'd be feeding yo ass to the crocodiles." He turned and laughed. "You a trip, Showbiz. Ain't no way you taking my father's throne from me. You got me all the way fucked up. Brooklyn out." His troops clicked their boots together and turned to follow him.

The rain began to come down harder. With every step that he took, the madder I became. When they filed away in their black Benz trucks, I turned to look over my father's tombstone. I mugged it. He'd given my birthright away, and because he had, there was a constant tug of war for what was rightfully mine. I wished he was alive, so I could kill his ass again.

***

"Showbiz, you've been in here for a minute, sitting in the dark. I know you got somethin' on your mind, but I need to ask you something that's fucking me up right now." Kalani stepped further into the room, holding a vanilla scented candle in her hand.

I was sitting on the edge of the bed with my head bowed. There was a syringe filled with heroin in my left hand and I was debating on backtracking by shooting it. It had been six months since I'd had any of the drug in my system. Six months since I'd stepped on to the Vega throne and started to get things in order. "What do you want, Kalani?"

"You see, that's the thing. The way you talk to me now, you make me feel like you don't like being around me. Have I worn out my welcome here? You can be honest with me."

"What are you talking about? Keep in mind that I got a whole list of shit on my brain and don't none of it involve that emotional shit. My brother coming for this throne, and I need to break his ass down. But at the same time, I don't want to crush his ass and lose the support of his mother. That bitch name rings bells all the way to Hong Kong, word to Jehovah, man."

Kalani stood in front of me. She popped back on her legs. "This will only take a minute, and then you can go back to your pondering." She knelt before me. "Showbiz, I need to know how you feel about me because I am tired of guessing."

I mugged her and hated the fact that she was so oblivious to everything that mattered. "Kalani, ain't a nigga alive that don't like a bitch that ain't on her game. You sit around this mafucka all day long doin' nothin'. You got all of the potential in the world, but you ain't doing shit wit' it. You just like to walk around this mansion strutting like your looks gon' keep you with your slot for the rest of your life. Bitch, get real, word up."

"So you're saying that I have worn out my welcome?"

I sighed. "Man, go find you something to do before I buss yo ass." I waved her off.

"As long as you know that I'ma fight yo ass back, I don't give a fuck what you try. Now I'm asking you a simple ass question, have I worn out my welcome here?"

"Man, I ain't never welcomed you to shit. What the fuck is you talkin' about? You smooth, but there is no value to you. You don't contribute shit to this empire, and you are easily forgotten. Every mafucka in my circle put in work, except you. Sooner or later, you gon' have to make a statement to me, or hell yeah, I'ma have to evict you as my bitch. Now get the fuck out of here."

She stood up and bowed her head. "Enough said. Wait, I will say this. I love you, Showbiz. These past few years with you have been everything to me. I appreciate you more than you will ever know. I'ma figure some things out, and then see if you'll respect me then. I got you. I know that I gotta put in some work, so let me start with this. I got the address to Tristian's mansion, and all of the places his bitch frequents. You wanna hurt him, you knock that bitch. He won't be able to cope, since he's all up her ass." She pulled out her phone and typed in the addresses and handed it to me. "You're welcome."

"How did you get this?"

"What you see is dead weight, and what I am is on point. You'll see. Good night, Showbiz." She left out of the room with me staring at her phone. I was wondering if I had gone too hard on her. After all, Kalani had been by my side at the worst of times. I wasn't tripping. I would make shit right later. For now, there were more important matters to attend to.

***

Three days later, Mecca and two of the Vega Bloods snatched up Perjah while she was headed into Walmart. She was thrown into the back of a black minivan and brought directly to me. When I pulled the black head covering off of her, she had tears streaming down her face, along with mascara. I knelt low and rubbed her cheek.

"So this is my sister-in-law. How are you doing gorgeous?" I ripped the duct tape off of her face. She yelped and tossed her head back.

"What are you going to do to me? Why am I here?" Her breathing was rapid.

"I gotta be honest with you, bitch, you basic as hell. I can't see why Tristian has been all up yo ass like you this major dime or somethin'."

144

"Why am I here, Showbiz?" She gave me a menacing look. Her lace front was coming undone, as if she'd been in a scuffle.

"Well, sis." I laughed. "It seems that your husband, Tristian, is looking forward to stepping back up on the Vega throne. That would make it crowded, seeing as I'm already sitting on this mafucka. Now, me personally, I would smash this nigga and all of those Buck Town Brooklyn niggas like roaches on the floors of Harlem, but me and his mother, well let's just say we are cordial. I need her, and she needs me. If I kill her son, I don't know how that would fair for me in the foreign world. And contrary to what most people believe, you can't survive in this game without strong foreign relationships."

Perjah rolled her eyes. "Damn, Showbiz, you are the worst kind. First Kalani, then the boy's mother. What's the matter with you?" She took a deep breath and blew it out. "I shouldn't be here right now. I am pregnant. Tristian will blow a gasket if he finds out how you've treated me. Release me at once."

"Perjah, you're not going anywhere until you help me figure out how to get your husband out of my fuckin' way."

"I don't even want him to have any parts with the Vegas. We already lost a daughter, and my parents, fuckin' with y'all. He doesn't need the money. We're straight. I don't know what your father has instilled in you boys, but y'all got a sick obsession with being the king of something. Don't you two understand that you aren't really the king of anything? You are a man. You are being used. Whenever those real powers that are in charge decide to get rid of y'all, they will, and the next idiot will take your slot. Wake the fuck up, or as they say, stay woke. Now release me. I gotta get home and make dinner."

I ran my hand along the side of her face. "Now I see why he likes you. You're feisty, and you got a lot of heart in you."

I stood up and pulled a Desert Eagle out of my belt. I grabbed her by the throat and stuffed it down her mouth. "Bitch, if you don't get your husband to give up his pursuit of this throne, I'ma smoke you and his bitch ass. You see how easy it was for me to get you. His punk ass security caught dome shots and wet up their windshields, and they didn't even see it coming. This is just a warning. I don't know what you gon' tell that nigga but squash this shit before it get real hectic. You hear me?"

Chapter 16

"You know what, Showbiz, go fuck yourself," she spat. "I ain't scared of you. To me, you ain't nothin' but a coward. You're weak. Any man that can kill a little girl, and watch his own son be murdered over some beef that was his own, ain't nothin' but a chicken. You got all of these people in Harlem fooled. You ain't tough. That nigga, Jimmy, used to kick your ass all the time, back in the day. Now his homeboy, Kammron, is really the one that's running Harlem. You're doing small things on the outskirts, according to my husband. Your whole life you wanted to be Tristian. He had the stronger mother, better morals, smarter. You've always been a follower, until most recently. Your father saw the same things in you that everybody else has been seeing this whole time. That's an incompetent little boy with self-esteem issues. So yeah, go fuck yourself."

"Well label me shocked and appalled." I stood up with my hand against my chest for dramatic effect. I slapped her so hard that she yelped and spit blood at the same time. "Watch yo' mouth when you talk to the Don."

She turned back to look at me. "If I was a man, I'd smoke you, kid. I ain't afraid of you. You're one of those punk men that beat women but would get your ass handed to you if you ever tried that with a real man. You're saying that you want my husband to step down and away from the Vega throne. Well I'm telling you that you're going to have to make him do it on your own. I refuse to cross him, or my daughter, like that. Piss off." She mugged me with hatred.

I grabbed her jaw and squeezed it. "You know what, bitch, I did kill yo punk ass daughter. I finished that li'l ho, bam, a blade right through her little heart. She screamed and kicked her little legs until they stopped. There was so much blood that..."

"Aww, fuck you, Showbiz. Fuck you. You rotten son of a bitch. I hate you. I hate you and one day you gon' get yours," she screamed.

I stood up. "Tie this bitch up and take her to the spot out in the Bronx. I got plans for her tough ass, word up." I smacked her again and walked away.

Mecca came alongside me while my troops were getting Perjah prepared to be transported. "Yo, you was just fuckin' wit' her, right? Like you really didn't kill that bitch's kid, did you?"

"Kinda, but it's a long story. Make sure they get her to the Bronx. I got some shit I gotta handle." I walked away from Mecca, leaving her standing there looking stupid.

Chapter 17

"I just don't understand, Showbiz. I had some of my best men trailing her, kid. I put mafuckas around her that were 'bout that life. Ain't no way my dudes get knocked off that easily and my pregnant wife get snatched up the way that she did, unless it was an inside job. No way." Tristian stood up and drank from his bottle of Hennessey.

We were at his three story house out in Brooklyn. After coming straight from Harlem, where the team finished wrapping up Perjah and transporting her to the Bronx, I got into that mode where I wanted to be over and done with the whole fight for the throne shit. I wanted to crush Tristian, and I was trying my best to find a way to do it without it affecting my plug with Deborah.

"Yo, kid, I think it was that nigga, Kammron, from the Coke Kings. No cap, I got some strong intel that says he is thinking about moving his troops out to Brooklyn after conquering Queens. He ain't seeing Bonkers as a threat, and that nigga feeling like you and I are divided. Word to Amelia, son might've been laying on shorty whole schedule for a minute now. You know the type."

Tristian looked at me. "So what's his endgame, then, Showbiz? He got Perjah, and now what?"

"Nigga, I don't know, but I say we sweat that bitch ass nigga and see what's good. I got the drop on a few of the places where he lays his head. In fact, that nigga Bonkers right here in Brooklyn. They still jammed pack because Bonkers know he can't fuck with Kammron. Why don't we smash Bonkers and then Kammron? Sooner or later, we gon' have to holler at both of them niggas anyway."

Tristian stood there for a moment lost in deep thought. He stopped and shook his head. "N'all, man, if I make the wrong move, Perjah could wind up losing her life. I would never be able to live with myself." He plopped down on the couch. "I'm glad my son is with my mother for two weeks. If he had been with Perjah, I would really be going through it right now." He drank from his bottle and downed a bunch of it. I thought to myself that this is why Tristian was never fit to be king of our bloodline. If it were me under the gun, I would've been out tearing up New York looking for my people. The murder rate would've been through the roof.

I sat across from him. "Tristian?"

He looked up. "What, man?"

"You acting like a bitch right now, son." I laughed.

"Yo, fuck you, Dunn. You don't know what I'm going through. Perjah is my whole world. Ever since she came into my life, it's been me and her. I don't know what the fuck to do without her." He drank some more of his bottle.

"You keep pushing. You said you wanna be king right? Well if that's the case, you gotta be ready to endure all types of shit like this. Suck it up. You a mafuckin' Vega."

He shook his head. "Yo, I know why this type of shit keeps happening to me. I'm a fraud, man, and the Bible says that we are to respect our parents, or our days will be shortened."

"What are you talking about?" I scooted to the edge of the sofa.

"I should've stopped her? I should've never let her poison our father. I should've never let her kill him slowly like that. Ever since I did, there ain't been nothing but tragedy and chaos." He fell to his knees and broke down.

I stood up. "Who poisoned pops?"

"My mother, kid. She the reason he had that cancer shit that took him out. Yo, I knew. I wanted the throne so bad that I didn't say shit, but I knew, and it's fuckin' me up." He started to cry so loud that I couldn't hear myself think.

I walked over to him and upped my .40 Glock. "Bitch, is you telling me the truth?"

He nodded. "Yeah, man. That's why I'm so fucked up right now. I have been seeing daddy in my dreams. He said that he gon come back and..."

I pushed him to the floor. He kept crying. "Yo, that's fucked up, B. You and yo mama are nuts." I left his home in a frenzy, and stormed out to the Bronx.

***

I opened the door to the locked room and stepped inside of it. Perjah looked up at me with her right wrist handcuffed to the bed.

"Aw shit, I already know why you here. You dirty son of a bitch."

I closed the door behind me and paced back and forth. My mind was all over the place. I kept hearing Tristian's confession. First Deborah was giving him the money to take over the throne, and then she was flat out poisoning Chico in order to get him out of the way sooner. She was more evil than I'd previously thought. I stopped in front of Perjah's bed. "Did you know?"

She tried to pull her dress down with one hand. "Did I know what?"

"Don't play wit' me, Perjah. Did you know that Deborah poisoned my father in order to get him out of the way so that Tristian could be king?"

She shook her head. "What are you talking about?"

My brain began to spin. *Why would Deborah take me overseas to get me plugged in with Khabir if she wanted Tristian to be king so bad? Why would she admit to giving him the money to help him conquer the Vega throne, but then not*

151

tell me about poisoning my father? Was it all a set up? Was she the one pulling the strings? And if so, what was her end game, I wondered.

"Look, Showbiz, I don't know what you got going on inside of your mind, but it doesn't have nothing to do with me or my unborn child. You need to man up and take up all of these things with Tristian."

"Shut up, bitch. Shut up. You getting on my mafuckin' nerves." I pulled the .40 Glock off of my belt and aimed it at her. "Ever since yo monka-ass came into the picture, it ain't been nothing but one problem after the next. I don't know what it is about you, but you are bad luck to the Vegas, you and your punk ass daughter."

"Hey, Showbiz, you need to calm down. Now I don't know what you're going through, but I assure you that I don't have nothin' to do with it. Now you have to let me go. I am innocent in all of this. Brittany was innocent in all of this, and so were my parents."

I shook my head. "Fuck them. What's so good about you anyway, huh? Why this nigga love you so much?" I stepped closer to the bed and leaned over her.

She scooted as far away as possible. "Here we go. Please, Showbiz. You need to go and take this up with your brother. This ain't got shit to do with me."

I tucked my gun into the small of my back. I needed to see what Tristian found so alluring about this basic ass bitch. I didn't get it, so it had to be the box. I yanked her dress backward and exposed her thighs. Her pink panties flashed me. Her thighs were thick and juicy.

"Showbiz, what are you getting ready to do to me? Whatever it is, I don't deserve it, and you know I don't." She whimpered, and once again, she tried to back away from me, until I yanked her ass back in place.

I climbed on the bed. "That nigga cheated to get the throne. On top of that, his punk ass mother was poisoning my father the whole time. Everything shady he got coming, he deserved. Since you are a part of him, you gotta take this L."

I jumped on top of her and yanked her panties down. She tried to keep her thighs together to prevent me from doing so, but it was of no use. I was too strong and too determined. When I got between her legs, she looked me straight in the eye. "You don't have to do this. I am innocent. Please."

Her pleas fell on deaf ears. I released my piece, and lined myself up. I peeled her thick lips apart and slid all the way inside of her until my nuts were resting on her ass. She felt hot as lava, and soft as velvet. Tight, I groaned. She punched at my chest, and screamed for me to get off of her. I started going, ignoring her once again. I grabbed her neck, started to plunge deep.

Then the room door burst open and Tristian stood in the doorway with a Glock Nine with a silencer on it. The barrel was smoking as if he'd just let off a bunch of shots. When he saw what I was doing to this wife, his eyes became menacing. Beside him was both Kalani and Mecca.

Kalani crossed her arms in front of her chest. "Yo, I told you this is what he would be doing to the bitch. This nigga ain't no good."

Mecca stepped forward. "You killed that girl's baby, Biz. Damn, why would you do that? I thought you were better than that. I can't fall under a nigga like you. You are too heartless. That was a little girl."

"Arrgh," Tristian growled and rushed me at full speed. He tackled me off of Perjah. He swung a right hook and connected with my jaw so hard that I grew dizzy. I fell to the floor with my pants around my knees, and my dick bobbing. I searched my waist for my gun and saw Tristian handing both his gun, and mine to Mecca.

"Yo, I promise to restore Harlem, Mecca, you got my word on that. And Kalani, thank you for telling me the truth about Brittany, and everything else. I know we had our differences, but I appreciate you." He turned back to me. "Nigga, get yo bitch ass up."

I was on my feet with my guards up. Dizzy but ready to rock and roll. I pulled up my pants with one hand, and got ready for his punk ass. He rushed me, swinging haymakers, fuckin' me up, but I was off of those Percs and I couldn't really feel shit. I caught his fist, and head butt him in the face. He flew backward, holding it. I knew this nigga couldn't fuck with my bidness. I had that pistol play and that Mike Tyson shit, too.

I rushed him and tackled him into the dresser. He hit his head on the wall. Blood skeet from it. He fell to his knee. We struggled, twisting and turning like crazy on the floor. That nigga was bleeding like a stuck pig. I loved it. I wound up on top of his soft ass, punching him over and over again with these Uptown knuckles. Bitch nigga talking bout he was gon' restore Harlem. I was Harlem. My second wind was kicking in. Perjah yelled for Tristian to fight back. It's fucked up when a nigga's bitch gotta tell him to do that.

He tried to get up, but I kept punching him, over and over. I roared. He fainted. I kept punching harder and harder. His blood popped into my face. I relished in the feel of it. Faster and faster, I punched, imagining him on the Vega's throne. His head ricocheted off of the ground with his eyes closed. I leaned down and bit a plug out of his face, ripping the flesh from his bone. I spit it out.

"I'm the king. Me, nigga. Just me." I bit another piece off. His blood dripped off of my chin. I stood up and stomped him, over and over and over. My Balenciagas were drenched with blood. My ankles were wet. Then I knelt and punched him savagely, over and over, all over again, while Perjah screamed for Mecca to shoot me.

I stood up and looked down on his body. His bone was completely visible on his face. Half of the structure was smashed in. I wiped my mouth and held my hand out to Mecca. "Goddess, give me the gun. Come on."

She backed up. "Showbiz, yo ass is crazy. I don't know what to think no more." She backed up some more.

"Girl, what the fuck is you doing? Shoot him. Shoot him now." Kalani urged, backing away as well. "He doesn't love either one of us. He's too crazy. Look at him."

"N'all, I love him too much. And that pancake shit ain't in me. I'm sorry, Showbiz, but I'm out of here." She turned to run out of the room and bumped smack dead into Kammron. She fell on her ass and dropped both guns. They fell into the hallway and slid down the floor. "Fuck."

Kalani smiled. "You finally got here. There he goes right there, daddy." She pointed at me. "That's yo' ass now, Showbiz. Yo punk ass trapped. Karma is a bitch. Can you see her?" She mugged me.

Kammron held a F&N in his hand. He held it straight out. "Yo, Mecca, y'all scared to murder this nigga? Shid, watch this." He aimed and I rushed him, and went right for the gun.

Boom. Boom. Boom. Boom.

I felt the first bullet knock the right side of my face off. It felt like the worst pain ever. I kept going at Kammron. The second bullet planted a hole in my throat. I stopped and twisted around. I saw a piece of my brain fall out of my skull. I struggled to breathe. I dropped to the carpet.

Kammron turned the gun on Mecca and bucked her four times. She jerked in the air with her face opened up and fell beside me. He aimed the gun at Perjah, and dumped five rounds into her body, then threw Kalani to the floor and finished her, as well.

"Can't trust a snake bitch that been setting her nigga up the whole time for his demise. You ain't worthy to be a Coke Queen." He spat at her.

I was still struggling to make it. My right leg kicked wildly. Then he squatted down and smiled.

"Poor Juanito Vega. You did all of the work for me. I been fuckin' wit Khabir for a long time already. Deborah was my old bitch. The Gomez fields belong to the Coke Kings, and the Vegas." He laughed and stuck his finger into one of the holes in my throat. He pulled it out and flicked the blood on me. "There can only be one King of New York, Showbiz, and that muthafucka ain't you, or Bonkers, or Tristian. Bitch nigga, it's me. It's Coke Kings or nothin'. Lights out." He placed the gun to my forehead and squeezed the trigger. Bullet after bullet entered into me before everything faded to black.

***

I guess when it came to the game, you had to always expect the unexpected. It was imperative that you lived by the code of trusting no man or no bitch. Karma always came back to get a nigga. And no matter what you thought you were getting away with, the game always had the last laugh.

I was Showbiz Vega. I died at twenty five, but I lived the life and reached the pentacle that most of you dope boys will never reach. I did what I did, and I was who I was. That bitch nigga, Kammron, got me in the end, or was it Kalani? Shit, it doesn't matter. I lost. I went on a terror spree, and will be remembered as a true legend. Long live the Vegas. The game was ours, and now it belonged to Kammron and the Coke Kings. It is what it is.

The End

Submission Guideline

Submit the first three chapters of your completed manuscript to ldpsubmissions@gmail.com, subject line: Your book's title. The manuscript must be in a .doc file and sent as an attachment. Document should be in Times New Roman, double spaced and in size 12 font. Also, provide your synopsis and full contact information. If sending multiple submissions, they must each be in a separate email.

Have a story but no way to send it electronically? You can still submit to LDP/Ca$h Presents. Send in the first three chapters, written or typed, of your completed manuscript to:

LDP: Submissions Dept
Po Box 944
Stockbridge, Ga 30281

DO NOT send original manuscript. Must be a duplicate.

Provide your synopsis and a cover letter containing your full contact information.

Thanks for considering LDP and Ca$h Presents.

<u>Coming Soon from Lock Down Publications/Ca$h Presents</u>

BOW DOWN TO MY GANGSTA
By **Ca$h**
TORN BETWEEN TWO
By **Coffee**
THE STREETS STAINED MY SOUL **II**
By **Marcellus Allen**
BLOOD OF A BOSS **VI**
SHADOWS OF THE GAME II
By **Askari**
LOYAL TO THE GAME **IV**
By **T.J. & Jelissa**
A DOPEBOY'S PRAYER **II**
By **Eddie "Wolf" Lee**
IF LOVING YOU IS WRONG... **III**
By **Jelissa**
TRUE SAVAGE **VII**
MIDNIGHT CARTEL III
DOPE BOY MAGIC IV
By **Chris Green**
BLAST FOR ME **III**
A SAVAGE DOPEBOY III
CUTTHROAT MAFIA II
By **Ghost**
A HUSTLER'S DECEIT III
KILL ZONE **II**

T.J. Edwards

BAE BELONGS TO ME III
A DOPE BOY'S QUEEN II
By **Aryanna**
CHAINED TO THE STREETS III
By **J-Blunt**
COKE KINGS IV
By **T.J. Edwards**
GORILLAZ IN THE BAY V
TEARS OF A GANGSTA II
De'Kari
THE STREETS ARE CALLING II
Duquie Wilson
KINGPIN KILLAZ IV
STREET KINGS III
PAID IN BLOOD III
CARTEL KILLAZ IV
DOPE GODS II
Hood Rich
SINS OF A HUSTLA II
ASAD
TRIGGADALE III
Elijah R. Freeman
KINGZ OF THE GAME V
Playa Ray
SLAUGHTER GANG IV
RUTHLESS HEART IV
By Willie Slaughter

160

THE HEART OF A SAVAGE III

By Jibril Williams

FUK SHYT II

By Blakk Diamond

THE DOPEMAN'S BODYGAURD II

By Tranay Adams

TRAP GOD II

By Troublesome

YAYO III

A SHOOTER'S AMBITION III

By S. Allen

GHOST MOB

Stilloan Robinson

KINGPIN DREAMS II

By Paper Boi Rari

CREAM

By Yolanda Moore

SON OF A DOPE FIEND II

By Renta

FOREVER GANGSTA II

GLOCKS ON SATIN SHEETS II

By Adrian Dulan

LOYALTY AIN'T PROMISED II

By Keith Williams

THE PRICE YOU PAY FOR LOVE II

DOPE GIRL MAGIC II

By Destiny Skai

TOE TAGZ III

By Ah'Million

CONFESSIONS OF A GANGSTA II

By Nicholas Lock

I'M NOTHING WITHOUT HIS LOVE II

By Monet Dragun

CAUGHT UP IN THE LIFE II

By Robert Baptiste

NEW TO THE GAME III

By **Malik D. Rice**

LIFE OF A SAVAGE III

By **Romell Tukes**

QUIET MONEY II

By **Trai'Quan**

THE STREETS MADE ME II

By **Larry D. Wright**

THE ULTIMATE SACRIFICE VI

By **Anthony Fields**

THE LIFE OF A HOOD STAR

By Ca$h & Rashia Wilson

Available Now

RESTRAINING ORDER **I & II**

By **CA$H & Coffee**

LOVE KNOWS NO BOUNDARIES **I II & III**
By **Coffee**
RAISED AS A GOON I, II, III & IV
BRED BY THE SLUMS I, II, III
BLAST FOR ME I & II
ROTTEN TO THE CORE I II III
A BRONX TALE I, II, III
DUFFEL BAG CARTEL I II III IV
HEARTLESS GOON I II III IV
A SAVAGE DOPEBOY I II
HEARTLESS GOON I II III
DRUG LORDS I II III
CUTTHROAT MAFIA
By **Ghost**
LAY IT DOWN **I & II**
LAST OF A DYING BREED
BLOOD STAINS OF A SHOTTA I & II III
By **Jamaica**
LOYAL TO THE GAME I II III
LIFE OF SIN I, II III
By **TJ & Jelissa**
BLOODY COMMAS I & II
SKI MASK CARTEL I II & III
KING OF NEW YORK I II,III IV V
RISE TO POWER I II III
COKE KINGS I II III
BORN HEARTLESS I II III IV

By **T.J. Edwards**

IF LOVING HIM IS WRONG…I & II

LOVE ME EVEN WHEN IT HURTS I II III

By **Jelissa**

WHEN THE STREETS CLAP BACK I & II III

THE HEART OF A SAVAGE I II

By **Jibril Williams**

A DISTINGUISHED THUG STOLE MY HEART I II & III

LOVE SHOULDN'T HURT I II III IV

RENEGADE BOYS I II III IV

PAID IN KARMA I II III

By **Meesha**

A GANGSTER'S CODE I &, II III

A GANGSTER'S SYN I II III

THE SAVAGE LIFE I II III

CHAINED TO THE STREETS I II

By J-Blunt

PUSH IT TO THE LIMIT

By **Bre' Hayes**

BLOOD OF A BOSS **I, II, III, IV, V**

SHADOWS OF THE GAME

By **Askari**

THE STREETS BLEED MURDER **I, II & III**

THE HEART OF A GANGSTA I II& III

By **Jerry Jackson**

CUM FOR ME I II III IV V

An **LDP Erotica Collaboration**

BRIDE OF A HUSTLA **I** **II & II**
THE FETTI GIRLS **I, II& III**
CORRUPTED BY A GANGSTA I, II III, IV
BLINDED BY HIS LOVE
THE PRICE YOU PAY FOR LOVE
DOPE GIRL MAGIC
By **Destiny Skai**
WHEN A GOOD GIRL GOES BAD
By **Adrienne**
THE COST OF LOYALTY I II III
By Kweli
A GANGSTER'S REVENGE **I II III & IV**
THE BOSS MAN'S DAUGHTERS I II III IV V
A SAVAGE LOVE **I & II**
BAE BELONGS TO ME I II
A HUSTLER'S DECEIT I, II, III
WHAT BAD BITCHES DO I, II, III
SOUL OF A MONSTER I II III
KILL ZONE
A DOPE BOY'S QUEEN
By **Aryanna**
A KINGPIN'S AMBITON
A KINGPIN'S AMBITION **II**
I MURDER FOR THE DOUGH
By **Ambitious**
TRUE SAVAGE I II III IV V VI
DOPE BOY MAGIC I, II, III

T.J. Edwards

MIDNIGHT CARTEL I II
By **Chris Green**
A DOPEBOY'S PRAYER
By **Eddie "Wolf" Lee**
THE KING CARTEL **I, II & III**
By **Frank Gresham**
THESE NIGGAS AIN'T LOYAL **I, II & III**
By **Nikki Tee**
GANGSTA SHYT **I II &III**
By **CATO**
THE ULTIMATE BETRAYAL
By **Phoenix**
BOSS'N UP **I , II & III**
By **Royal Nicole**
I LOVE YOU TO DEATH
By Destiny J
I RIDE FOR MY HITTA
I STILL RIDE FOR MY HITTA
By **Misty Holt**
LOVE & CHASIN' PAPER
By **Qay Crockett**
TO DIE IN VAIN
SINS OF A HUSTLA
By **ASAD**
BROOKLYN HUSTLAZ
By **Boogsy Morina**
BROOKLYN ON LOCK I & II

By **Sonovia**

GANGSTA CITY

By **Teddy Duke**

A DRUG KING AND HIS DIAMOND I & II III

A DOPEMAN'S RICHES

HER MAN, MINE'S TOO I, II

CASH MONEY HO'S

By Nicole Goosby

TRAPHOUSE KING **I II & III**

KINGPIN KILLAZ I II III

STREET KINGS I II

PAID IN BLOOD **I II**

CARTEL KILLAZ I II III

DOPE GODS

By **Hood Rich**

LIPSTICK KILLAH **I, II, III**

CRIME OF PASSION I II & III

By **Mimi**

STEADY MOBBN' **I, II, III**

THE STREETS STAINED MY SOUL

By **Marcellus Allen**

WHO SHOT YA **I, II, III**

SON OF A DOPE FIEND

Renta

GORILLAZ IN THE BAY **I II III IV**

TEARS OF A GANGSTA

DE'KARI

T.J. Edwards

TRIGGADALE I II

Elijah R. Freeman

GOD BLESS THE TRAPPERS I, II, III

THESE SCANDALOUS STREETS I, II, III

FEAR MY GANGSTA I, II, III

THESE STREETS DON'T LOVE NOBODY I, II

BURY ME A G I, II, III, IV, V

A GANGSTA'S EMPIRE I, II, III, IV

THE DOPEMAN'S BODYGAURD

Tranay Adams

THE STREETS ARE CALLING

Duquie Wilson

MARRIED TO A BOSS... I II III

By Destiny Skai & Chris Green

KINGZ OF THE GAME I II III IV

Playa Ray

SLAUGHTER GANG I II III

RUTHLESS HEART I II III

By Willie Slaughter

FUK SHYT

By Blakk Diamond

DON'T F#CK WITH MY HEART I II

By Linnea

ADDICTED TO THE DRAMA I II III

By Jamila

YAYO I II

A SHOOTER'S AMBITION I II

168

By S. Allen
TRAP GOD
By Troublesome
FOREVER GANGSTA
GLOCKS ON SATIN SHEETS
By Adrian Dulan
TOE TAGZ I II
By Ah'Million
KINGPIN DREAMS
By Paper Boi Rari
CONFESSIONS OF A GANGSTA
By Nicholas Lock
I'M NOTHING WITHOUT HIS LOVE
By Monet Dragun
CAUGHT UP IN THE LIFE
By Robert Baptiste
NEW TO THE GAME I II
By **Malik D. Rice**
Life of a Savage I II
By **Romell Tukes**
LOYALTY AIN'T PROMISED
By Keith Williams
Quiet Money
By **Trai'Quan**
THE STREETS MADE ME
By **Larry D. Wright**
THE ULTIMATE SACRIFICE I, II, III, IV, V

T.J. Edwards

KHADIFI
By **Anthony Fields**
THE LIFE OF A HOOD STAR
By Ca$h & Rashia Wilson

BOOKS BY LDP'S CEO, CA$H

TRUST IN NO MAN

TRUST IN NO MAN 2

TRUST IN NO MAN 3

BONDED BY BLOOD

SHORTY GOT A THUG

THUGS CRY

THUGS CRY 2

THUGS CRY 3

TRUST NO BITCH

TRUST NO BITCH 2

TRUST NO BITCH 3

TIL MY CASKET DROPS

RESTRAINING ORDER

RESTRAINING ORDER 2

IN LOVE WITH A CONVICT

LIFE OF A HOOD STAR

Coming Soon

BONDED BY BLOOD 2

BOW DOWN TO MY GANGSTA

T.J. Edwards